OF A

MAD
BRAIN

SCOTT DONNELLY

WeirdDarknessPublishing.com

Copyright © 2022, Scott Donnelly
All rights reserved
ISBN 979-8508095765

In late 2020 and early 2021, Darren Marlar of the Weird Darkness Podcast told a few of my stories on his show. For an indie writer to hear their work told so professionally and fantastically to such a massive audience - is surreal. It put me in a realm where so many people have been able to listen to and hopefully enjoy the horror tales I have woven. I quickly became a fan of Weird Darkness, and it didn't take long to see what a loyal following it has. I want to personally thank Mr. Marlar for all he does to scare us, entertain us, and take our minds away from reality for a short while each day. Also, for all he does for those who suffer from anxiety and depression. And to all the Weird Darkness Weirdos who have spent their own time listening to the few stories of mine, even if you didn't like them, I want you to know just how much your time means to me, as well as the other indie writers that you've made feel so proud.

Stay weird!
-Scott

SCOTT DONNELLY

PART ONE
VOID OF ALL LIFE

*I*t is a house that calls you. A house of darkness that will fulfill the desires of a mad brain. It is a house that haunts you with its ghosts; *your* ghosts. They'll scratch and claw through your fragile hide, bringing madness bubbling to the surface. Come see the ghosts for yourself.

I just stared at the paper in my hands that contained these words. They were elegantly typed on a clean sheet of white paper. I picked up the torn envelope from the kitchen table and looked at it *again* for a return address. I hadn't seen one upon my initial glance, and this time wasn't any different.

Weird, I thought. At this point I assumed the letter had been mistakenly put in my mailbox. The regular postman was off on his honeymoon, so a substitute carrier could have easily made the mistake; it happens. Plus, besides my home address, there was no name on the envelope to accompany it. We'd only moved into this house in the Summer Glen subdivision a year before, so the letter might have been meant for any number of previous residents.

I stuffed it back into the envelope, scribbled '*wrong address*' on it, and shoved it vertically between the toaster and coffee pot, where it joined some other letters and papers that I needed to get around to eventually. Kayla, my wife, hated my vertical paper stockpile. She cringed every time she saw it, but for some reason never did anything about it herself. It made me feel like I had more time to take care of it, so "*eventually*" is when I'd take care of it.

I left the kitchen, where the smell of bacon still filled the air from breakfast, and I lingered by the bookshelf. I'd read almost my entire collection, but the few that were left that I hadn't gotten around to continued to get beat out by the likes of Steinbeck, Lovecraft and Poe. Sometimes a comfort read sounded better than a new adventure. That line of thinking had kind of mirrored its way into my life as well. I was forty-two and not getting any younger. Comfort was winning in more parts of my life than I liked to admit. Hooded sweatshirts and windbreaker pants were still in as a go-to weekend getup as far as I was concerned. And a loose pair of jeans and a golf tee for the office worked just fine for me. Reruns of Seinfeld beat any new sitcom they could create, and even popping in a DVD instead of searching through a plethora of streaming options was favorable. The world had become such a fast-paced, digital haven that - although fascinating - I just couldn't keep up with.

"Dad! Move!" my son yelled at me. I turned from the bookshelf and saw Mark standing behind me, aiming his iPhone in my direction. He lowered the phone and repeated: "Move. You're in the shot."

"What shot?" I said. I turned around and saw one of our skull Halloween decorations sitting on the bookshelf. Fake blood was oozing from its eyes and dripping down onto the wood. "What are you doing?" I asked, annoyed by his confusing teenage antics.

Mark sighed loudly and stormed over, shoving the phone into his pocket. He grabbed a nearby rag and wiped the blood up from the skull and wooden shelf.

"What are you doing?" I repeated, more annoyed now that he chose to answer the first time in a waspish mien.

"Trying to make a Tik Tok video."

"A what?"

Mark smirked. "Come on, Dad, you've heard of Tik Tok. You're not *that* old, are you?" He finished wiping the blood from the bookshelf and dryly said, "This skull is going to be hilariously singing *The Monster Mash* all over the house. Even in the backyard."

In Mark's defense, I *had* heard of Tik Tok. But in *my* defense, that was the extent of my knowledge. I didn't know what it did, or where it was. And for the life of me, I didn't know what any of that had to do with a singing skull.

Mark tossed the bloodied rag over his shoulder, grabbed the skull and scurried out of the room. Tik Tok, challenges, memes...I loved what technology had done for the world, but some of this stuff had just gone too far; not to mention completely over my head.

I lay in bed with Kayla that night. She was reading another one of her young adult fantasy books that seemed to still be so popular, and I had one finger on the remote, continuously flipping through the endless apps on the TV across the room. It was hard to see the words from where I was laying, so I was trying to make my decision by the thumbnail images alone.

"Oh," Kayla abruptly said, laying her book down, "I need you to fix the railing on the back deck tomorrow. My parents will be over later this week and I was thinking about having a bonfire out back. The last thing I need is for my dad to go plunging off the side of the deck when he does his *leaning* thing."

"Sure," I said. I didn't say anything else after that. There was always something that needed fixed around the house. A railing, a kitchen drawer, tightening door knobs - I was starting to think my life had become too comfortable, repetitive.

I decided to just turn the TV off and I rolled to my side. I could hear Kayla turning the pages of her book as I drifted through thoughts of how boring my life actually was. I felt like I was accomplishing nothing. I was a faithful husband, a great father, and the hard-working breadwinner for my family. I wouldn't change any of that. But I did need something else. Something to re-energize my existence.

The next day I arrived at work with a coffee in hand and new motivation in the back of my mind. The library in town that I ran had been there for decades and underwent some remodeling at least once every couple of years. This year just happened to be a big one - they had knocked out the cafe near the entrance and were installing a daycare center for children. I was the one who signed off on the final papers to give them the go ahead, but I still had reservations about the project. The library was supposed to be quiet. Children were not quiet. I could already hear the complaints coming in.

After we opened the doors for the day, with the construction area safely blocked off, I fielded complaint after complaint from the patrons who were there to either study or do research. "The drilling is too loud," "The construction guys were looking at me funny", "There's too much dust and I can't concentrate" - those were just a few of them. I knew the construction created a distraction, but there was nothing I could do about it. I apologized to seven or eight patrons before my lunch break arrived. I sat down to eat my brown-bagged sandwich and ziplocked bag of chips, and any motivation I had brought into work with me that morning had completely evaporated. I stared into space as I chewed and swallowed my lunch.

"Idiots!" a young man's voice shouted loudly from behind me in the office. I turned around and saw Tim, one of my employees, slamming a small stack of books down onto his desk. Tim was fairly new, some sort of extended family friend on Kayla's side who desperately needed work. His father had recently passed away and fate put him here with me. Tim sat down, pulled his desk drawer open, and grabbed a roll of clear packing tape from inside.

I set down the last couple bites of my sandwich and walked over to him.

"What's wrong, Tim?" I asked.

He looked up at me. "No respect, Mr. Morris." Tim flipped open the book at the top of his stack to reveal several torn pages. I nodded and shared his frustration. *Some people.*

Tim tried to tear off some of the packing tape, but it folded in and stuck to itself. I could see him becoming more and more irritated.

"Can I help?" I asked.

"Thanks," Tim said without an ounce of hesitation. He methodically removed the top three books from the stack and set them aside. He lifted the bottom three and handed them to me. I immediately stared at the matte cover that faced me. The book was called *Ghost House* and prominently featured a decrepit old house with the faded image of a creepy-as-hell haunted doll's face above it in the dark clouds. I just stood there and stared at it. The image bothered me. I could feel my heart start to pick up its pace and then for some strange reason I thought of the letter I had grabbed out of the mailbox a day earlier.

"Mr. Morris, are you okay?" Tim asked, snapping me out of the aberrant trance that had tamed my senses.

"Yes," I said. I gathered my thoughts and carried the books back to my desk. I finished my lunch before I taped the torn pages back together.

My shift ended, and Ashley, the head librarian, took over until close. I drove home, still feeling a bit uneasy, but unable to place exactly what was wrong. The *Ghost House* book cover bothered me earlier in the day, but that couldn't have been what my subconscious was still carrying. It didn't make sense; my entire body had been pricked with anxiety since lunch.

I pulled into the Summer Glen subdivision and onto my street. The wind had picked up, ripping more and more of the dead leaves off the trees and sending them spinning through the air before gently landing in the grass or on the road. It was only a matter of time before all the trees would be bare and the cold weather would arrive. As I got older, I dreaded the cold like never before. It hurt my bones and stung my skin. I shook my head as I pulled into the driveway, annoying myself - I was starting to feel like my dad or grandfather. Grumpiness seemed to be hereditary in the Morris family.

I grabbed the mail before I went inside. Kayla was cooking chili on the stove, and Mark was nowhere to be seen. I kissed my wife, giving her a tight hug immediately after.

"I'm glad you're home," Kayla said.

I kissed her one more time, an innocent peck on the lips, and said, "Me, too." I looked around as the invisible teenager became more obvious. "Where's Mark?"

"At Jennie's house. He promised he'd be back before dinner was on the table, but this chili is in simmer mode now, so his time is just about up."

I sighed hard out of my nose. Mark was becoming famous for his late arrivals. You give the boy an inch and he takes a mile. I dropped the mail on the table, pulled my phone out and sent him a quick text telling him dinner was ready and he'd better get home immediately.

Kayla fingered through the mail. She pushed aside the junk, separated out the lone bill, and picked up a letter that had found its way to the bottom of the pile.

"What's this?" she asked. Kayla turned the letter around and my stomach sank.

It was a white envelope with only our address written on it. I snatched it out of her hand and looked it all over for a return address, but there was none to be found.

"Sam? What is it?" she repeated.

I was aware I hadn't answered her, but I didn't know what it was. I was hoping it wasn't another one of those ghost letters. It was weird enough not knowing what that first one was all about, and I could only imagine that knowing what it meant could be even more strange.

I ripped the envelope open and pulled out another piece of crisp computer paper, neatly folded over once. I unfolded it and a small 2x2 photo fell out and onto the floor. Kayla picked it up as I read the neatly typed words on the page:

In this house of ghosts, truths will be discovered and lives will be changed, for life in this house is nothing more than an appraisal.

This letter confused me even more than the first one did. My mind raced every which way, but I couldn't figure it out. *It has to be meant for someone else*, I thought as I looked back at the address on the envelope. It was our address. But the lack of any name continued to baffle me.

"What is this place?" Kayla asked, handing me the small photo that had fallen from the letter. I cautiously took it from her and looked at it. It was a black and white image of an eerie-looking gothic castle. It was night time in the photo and the blackness was so oversaturated that it made the details of the castle almost impossible to identify. There was nothing else in the photo. No date or names, no location - it was the strangest thing.

I finally answered my wife. "I don't know what this is. We got one yesterday, too," I said, grabbing the first one out from between the coffee pot and toaster. I handed it to Kayla, and she read it. She then took the one from my hands and read it as well.

She was just as clueless as I was.

"A joke, maybe?" she said.

I shrugged. "Maybe."

Right then, Mark burst in through the back door attached to the kitchen. He closed the door and looked at us, completely out of breath. He then looked to the table where the dinner had not been dished out yet, and smirked.

"Made it," he huffed.

The three of us ate chili for dinner, and the letters and picture of the castle quickly became the topic of conversation. I insisted they were meant for our house's former residents, Kayla seemed to think it was some sort of prank, but Mark had a very modern, Generation-Z angle.

"It's some sort of throwback viral marketing," he proclaimed. "Using a letter gives it a vintage effect which may be a clue as to what they're marketing."

"Wouldn't that just be regular marketing though?" I asked. "Lots of places and companies advertise through the mail."

Mark arrogantly chuckled. "No, Dad, the cryptic nature alone makes it modern, a la a form of viral marketing from the internet. It's not signed, it's not dated, the inclusion of Dracula's castle - not to mention it's not addressed to anyone in particular. That means it's completely random. Some company probably sent out a mass mailing of these across the city, maybe the state. I bet someone on Reddit has already started a thread on this."

"Reddit?" I asked.

Mark rolled his eyes, and I already felt older before he said anything. "Online forums. These types of things really get people talking. It's kind of cool."

I pulled the photo of the castle across the table and looked at it. "Does this place look familiar to either of you? Is it a landmark somewhere?"

Mark shrugged. "Where was the letter postmarked from?"

I grabbed the torn envelopes and looked for the postage. I looked at the front, and then the back. There was no postage. No stamps, no postmarks, nothing. How had I not noticed that before?

Mark grew giddy when he realized this. "Man, Dad, someone put these in our mailbox. Someone was outside our house, physically giving these to us."

Right then, the gears in my head began to shift direction. No longer was I confused about the letters, but now I was concerned for the safety of my family. Someone putting the letters in our mailbox, two days in a row, meant that person knew who he or she was giving them to. We were targets for...something.

A storm moved in that night, creating the atmosphere for the week of Halloween that you'd normally only see in movies. The thunder was loud and the lightning was frantic. The wind pounded the shutters outside our bedroom window, creating a sleepless environment. Well, for me at least. Kayla could sleep through a category five hurricane.

Even if there wasn't such a violent storm attacking us from outside, I wouldn't have been able to sleep. The letters were bothering me. The photo was bothering me. Rustling out from the depths of my brain, the faded image of the haunted baby doll on the cover of *Ghost House* began to make my chest flutter.

I rolled onto my side and closed my eyes, trying to erase the haunting images of the doll. As the doll left my consciousness, the castle appeared in all of its gothic glory. When the castle faded away, a woman's blood-curdling scream ripped my eyelids back open. I sat straight up in bed and listened to the thunder crashing over the top of the house. It rattled the pictures on the wall as well as a grouping of Kayla's perfume bottles on the dresser. Kayla was still asleep, only barely adjusting herself after the enormous boom. One of the picture frames hanging over Kayla's vanity dropped from its nail and broke on the ground.

I hopped out of bed and rushed over to it, turning on a small lamp nearby. I picked up the frame and saw the glass insert had only broken in two and didn't shatter into hundreds of little chips and shards. I looked at the picture in my hand. Mark was only four or five years old in it. He sat on a picnic blanket between Kayla and I at a park, and Kayla's sister Madison photobombed from the right with a huge and ornery smile on her face and her signature white-framed Looney Tunes sunglasses upon her head. The way the glass had cracked separated Madison from the rest of us.

The bedroom door creaked open, letting light in from down the hall. I stood up fast to see Mark standing there in sweatpants and a t-shirt, rubbing his eyes.

"What did you do, Dad?" Mark groggily asked.

"Nothing," I whispered. "The thunder shook the castle picture off the wall."

"What?" Mark asked.

I didn't realize I had said *castle* until a moment later and then corrected myself. "The picnic picture, I mean." I held it up for him to see. He nodded, still wondering why I had said "castle" first. *I* didn't even know.

As Mark turned to leave the doorway, I briskly followed him into the hall and quietly pulled the bedroom door shut. It clicked, and Mark turned around to see me.

"Is there a way to search for the castle online without knowing the location?" I asked.

Mark's dead stare turned into a grin. "Uh, yeah. You can do a reverse image search."

Finally, I was getting somewhere. "Let me get it," I said. As I descended the stairs, I could feel Mark's eyes affixed on me, probably wondering why I needed to know right then. I didn't have an answer for that.

We sat together in Mark's room at his computer. I watched as he whizzed through the screens with ease and was instantly brought back to a time when I was a young kid and the extent of my electronic knowledge was blowing into the undercarriage of a Nintendo cartridge. No matter how much of a myth that act is played off as now, there's no doubt it worked.

"Thanks for doing this," I said.

Mark smirked arrogantly again. "Technology isn't all that bad, right Dad?"

"It's fascinating," I said. But I wouldn't give him any more than that. I still found more trouble in it than good. But again, maybe that was my age talking.

I noticed Mark's attention to the computer drifted and he now gave an awkward look to the shelf above his desk. The skull he was using for his video sat up on it with the bloodied rag next to it still. Mark swallowed hard and then returned his attention. He took a picture of the castle photograph with his phone and airdropped it onto his laptop. *Okay, that's pretty cool*, I thought.

With a few more clicks and swipes, he had traced back the image before I even knew what was happening. I leaned in closer and looked at the plethora of castle images on the screen.

"That's it," Mark said. He sat back in his seat, satisfied with himself. I turned the computer toward me more and looked through the images. They were all of the same black and white structure as in my photo. Some of them were taken at night, some during the day. The daylight photos made the castle less ominous, and more regal. But the night photos returned it to being almost haunted. It looked like something from a movie. It was large, sat tucked behind trees in a dense forest, and a moat or stream seemed to surround it in some of the images.

"Where is this place?" I asked.

Mark didn't answer. I looked at him, but he was once again focused on the skull. I noticed his breathing was slightly elevated, like he was nervous or anxious. "Mark?"

Mark came back to reality and clicked into one of the images and a new window opened. Castle Shade appeared in bold letters, subtitled with Shade Family Laboratory. I scrolled down, skimming the article on the page. Castle Shade was located in upstate New York, hidden deep in the Catskill Mountains. It was owned by the Shade family and was in the midst of its fourth generation of Shade owners and operators.

I clicked into a link about the Shade family. The land was bought cheaply in the 1890s, the castle was erected in 1900, and it had been the home of the Shade Family Laboratory ever since. I squinted, trying to find out *anything* else, but the information was vague and limited.

Mark yawned very loudly in my ear, and I took the hint. Standing up from the chair, I said, "Can you print me some of this information?"

He nodded his head while exhausting yet another loud and irritating yawn.

"Thanks. Goodnight," I said as I left his room. As I closed the door, I saw Mark stand up and drape the bloodied rag over the skull. The door latched and I stood there for a moment, curious about Mark's attentiveness to the skull. He seemed...bothered by it. *Strange.*

25

Thunder still rumbled outside, but much more faint than it had been. When I returned to my bed, I was finally able to sleep.

My eyes ripped open to the sound of Kayla hustling into the bedroom. I sat up and saw the room was alive with the morning light coming through the unfurled curtains. Kayla rushed to the closet and rummaged through it.

"What's wrong?" I asked.

"Madison," my wife anxiously said. "She's missing."

"Missing?" I exclaimed, briefly thinking that I may have still been asleep.

"For two days now. Wasn't it nice of my family to tell me?" Kayla angrily and sarcastically quipped, tossing shirts, pants, underwear and makeup in a duffle bag. "I *have* to go help. She could be dead."

I was thrown by the suddenness of it all, but Madison being *dead* seemed like a darkly fanciful presumption. It wasn't like Kayla to think *that* drastically.

"Mark's coming with me. Can you get off work?" Kayla asked. "I need to be there in case they find a body."

"Of course," I said, placing her morbid and out-of-character assumptions aside. "Wait...Ashley's out of town. I'm the only manager."

Kayla nodded. She was clearly disappointed, but being a former manager herself, I could tell she understood that kind of problem. "I'll call you when we get there," she said.

Kayla zipped up the bag and hurried over to kiss me on the head. "Love you," she said as she raced out of the room.

"Love you. Keep me posted!" I responded. She was too far away to hear it, but it was a habit we'd gotten into. You never know when the last time you'll see someone is.

"*She screamed,*" a small voice whispered to me. I looked to the vanity where I assumed the voice had come from, and saw the nail on the wall from where the picture had fallen overnight. I climbed out of bed and approached the broken picture that I'd left sitting on the vanity. The crack had separated Madison from the rest of us after the thunderous rattling had sent it crashing to the floor.

"She screamed," I quietly agreed with the disembodied whisper, remembering the blood-curdling scream that awoke me in the night.

I dressed for the day and had a bowl of Cheerios. Mark had come through for me, leaving a few printed pages about the castle out on the counter. I leafed through them, and just as I had hoped, one of them actually had an address.

I did my own search after coming across those details and was able to screenshot directions to the castle. It was only a two hour drive. Kayla would be roughly two hours away in Pennsylvania with her family. I figured I had plenty of time to drive to Castle Shade, see what I could see, and get back in time. Ashley wasn't out of town, so I felt a little guilty for lying to my wife. But I just needed to see this place for myself; the intrigue had me gripped. It was a nagging itch that I *needed* to scratch.

With fresh coffee in my travel mug and nineties rock on the radio, I hit the road for Castle Shade.

The drive was peaceful. I was able to zone out and enjoy the autumn scenery. A sea of orange and red trees made up a bulk of the waving Catskills, and with my windows down, the cool scent of damp leaves filled the car.

I cruised through the winding roads, singing along to the music I grew up with and thinking about my destination. It was so mysterious how I was somehow the recipient of these odd letters.

I thought back to the first letter. *It is a house that calls you.* Indeed it was. *It is a house that haunts you with its ghosts; your ghosts.* This was the intriguing part to me. What ghosts? *Come see the ghosts for yourself.* Just as the letter suggested, I was on my way to do just that.

The run-of-the-mill existence I found myself living in, day in and day out, was in desperate need of an arousing thrill. And tracking down this castle, and everything it stood for, was exactly the thrill I craved.

Something caught my eye in the rearview mirror and I looked up into it. Nothing was there. I turned around and briefly looked into the backseat. Nothing.

I swung back and faced the road that slid underneath my car like an accelerated conveyor belt, and I smirked. I imagined that doll sitting in the backseat. Its eyes were wide and white, soulless and cryptic as if it held on dearly to a forbidden secret. I could even hear it laughing and cackling like an ornery demon. My smirk vanished and was replaced by a creeping sense of dread. I turned off the music and continued to drive through the mountains in silence, occasionally looking into my rearview. I even angled it down so I could have the entire backseat in view. I don't even know why I smirked to begin with. Just because I *knew* what it was up to? There was *nothing* funny about that doll.

It is a house that calls you. A house of darkness that will fulfill the desires of a mad brain.

Who were the Shade family? Why create cryptic letters? Was I randomly chosen? Specifically chosen? If so, how did the Shade family know about me? Did I know them? These were the questions that began to pepper my brain as I hit the final stretch of my drive. I pulled onto a gravelly road with no street sign, but I was certain it was the road specified on the map I had screenshotted. It led me through a more heavily wooded area than the rest of what I had traveled through thus far. The air was cooler, the trees made everything seem darker, and the road was wet as if it had rained here but not out on the other roads.

"Strange," I softly said to myself as I reduced my speed considerably and slowly steered around an abrupt sharp bend. My eyes shot open and I slammed on my brakes immediately. My car skidded to a stop, shaking over the rocky surface of the road. When it finally came to a rest, I realized just how close I was to hitting a metal gate.

I turned the car off and climbed out. The air outside was cold and dewy. The scent of a fire burning somewhere in the distance crept into my nose. Birds chirped in the wilderness that surrounded me and the buzzing of cicadas grew louder by the second.

I approached the gate that blocked the road. The white paint that once covered it was almost completely gone, now revealing an ocherous rust beneath it. The gate closed from one side of the road, but didn't connect or latch onto anything else. I pulled on it and was able to open the path once more.

I looked around into the woods with a familiar sense of dread coming over me. I felt like I was being watched. My heart rate picked up and I hurried back to my car.

Closing the door hard, I tried to calm myself before I started the ignition again. I closed my eyes and took a deep breath. After I exhaled, I once again heard a soft whispering voice.

"*Welcome,*" it ominously said.

My eyes shot back open, and I immediately knew where to look. The doll sat in the center of the backseat, its head tilted downward at an awkward angle and its body rested laxly against the back seat. The eyes were so white, so vacant of anything natural or living; they frightened me. I started the car and forcibly pushed the mirror the opposite way. I didn't want to look at it.

My car crawled the rest of the way, crunching the small rocks beneath the tires. And finally, revealing itself small bits at a time around the bend, Castle Shade sat before me. A moat surrounded it with a fragile wooden bridge that stretched across the width of water.

I knew better than to put my car on it, so I pulled off into a small grassy area just before the bridge and turned off the ignition. I climbed out and locked the door before putting the keys in my pocket. I zipped my jacket up and slowly approached the bridge, keeping my attention focused on the castle that sat just beyond it.

It looked just like it did in the pictures Mark found online, but seeing the perplexing monstrosity in person felt surreal; like finally meeting a celebrity that you've spent years watching on movie screens. Being October, and Halloween only days away, it was also hard not to compare the structure I was looking at to the massive dwellings in *Dracula* or *House on*

Haunted Hill. Castle Shade seemed like it was ripped straight from a classic horror film.

The ashen stones it was constructed of were slick and glazed with a velvety moss. It towered in front of me with at least three floors that I could see. Dark windows were placed sporadically on all visible sides and what looked like an empty bell tower was erected near the back of the castle.

I took a step onto the bridge and felt first hand just how fragile it was. It creaked upon my first step and only continued to lament as I made my way across. On the other side, the air was different. A notable chill surged through my body, springing to life scores of goosebumps and bristling hairs. I kept my attention forward as I made my concluding steps to the front entrance of the castle.

Come see the ghosts for yourself.

As the final line from the first letter repeated in my head, I found myself knocking on the castle's wooden door. Birds erupted loudly from the trees around me as I knocked. As they flew off, their frantic chirps grew faint and then non-existent. The cicadas had quieted, as did everything else. I was surrounded only by a haunting silence.

In the overgrown bushes to my left, I saw a bicycle. It was a mountain bike, still with a new shine. The red color was bright, the tires seemed strong — it looked out of place considering the rest of the environment I found myself in.

Is someone else here? I thought. I hadn't seen any sign of anyone else until this point. Even the gate down the road was still closed. Although if someone was on a bike, or even on foot, it wouldn't have been that hard to just go around it.

I knocked again and this time the door loosened and cracked open about a half an inch. It probably hadn't been closed all the way to begin with, and my knocking had jostled it from an unsecure position. I leaned in and tried to look inside but it was too dark.

"Hello?" I called out. My voice echoed inside. I waited in silence, hoping for an answer, but there was none coming. I looked down at my feet and watched as a wispy white fog began to seep out from inside the castle. I swallowed hard as the dread began to tingle throughout my body again.

Had I made the right decision by coming here? In the middle of the woods, standing in front of what I now assumed to be just an abandoned castle, the revelation of my having fallen for a prank was too hard to ignore. I had made the wrong decision. Now my sister-in-law was missing and I wasn't there to help. Guilt began to flush the dread from my body and I pulled my phone from my pocket. I dialed Kayla's number and she answered immediately. She was crying.

"Sam?" she sobbed.

"Hey, honey," I said, beginning the walk back to my car. "I can come after all."

"Great," Kayla sniveled. "There's a search party being organized right now."

A search party? My heart sank. This was serious. This wasn't just one of her drunken one-night stands that got around in the family gossip chain. Madison could really be in danger.

"Kayla," I began, but couldn't find the right words. I was sorry, guilty and not by my wife's side during such a horrible time for her. "I'll be there as soon as I can."

Kayla just cried on the other line. "I love you," I said. She tried to say it back, but couldn't speak. I hung up so she didn't have to say anything. She was hurting and I needed to be with her.

Before I stepped onto the bridge, I heard the castle's door creak loudly. I stopped and swung around. The door was wide open, and in the ghostly mist that whirled out from inside the castle stood a woman.

"Hello?" she said.

I just stood there, staring back at the woman in the castle's doorway, not knowing what to make of her. She was young, maybe in her late twenties or early thirties. She was easy on the eyes but looked tired. Her face was pale and she appeared nervous or even confused by my presence.

She glanced quickly down at the red mountain bike in the bushes and then back at me. I assumed it was her's by the suspicious glimpse she took. She obviously lived close enough to Castle Shade to just hop on a bike. That meant she was familiar with the area, and probably the castle itself.

"Hello," I finally responded. She seemed harmless enough, but life experience told me you can't trust someone based on their looks alone. "Are you part of the Shade family?"

The girl appeared confused. "No..." she said.

"You don't work or live here?" I asked.

She didn't answer my question, but instead asked one of her own. "Do you?"

I shook my head. "No. I'm just...visiting."

"Who lives here?" she asked.

"The Shade family," I said. "Well, that's what I gathered from online at least."

She nodded, accepting what I told her as truth. I didn't know her from Adam, nor did she me. She had no reason to trust what I was telling her. And trust goes both ways.

"What are you doing here?" I asked. "I mean, since you don't know who lives here."

I could see doubt in her eyes now. She was unsure of me. But her desire for an answer proved stronger than her uncertainty. She pulled a pleated piece of paper from her jeans pocket. She meticulously unfolded it and looked at whatever was on it. Then, she began to walk toward me.

I stood my ground, but remained wary. Again, her appearance was innocent enough, but for all I knew, *she* was the one who had lured me here. As she walked closer, I was able to get a better look at her. She was about a foot smaller than I was, thin and now appeared more than likely to be not significantly older than my son.

She stopped at arms length from me and handed me the paper. I accepted it from her and looked at the typed words on the page. It was identical to the first letter I had received.

I looked up from the paper and nodded to her. "I got the same thing. I got a second one too with a picture of this place."

"Me too," she said. Her voice was small and soft. "I'm Becca Brown," she said.

"Sam," I said, smart enough to not give her my last name.

We both looked at the castle, wondering now more than ever, why were we here? I noticed Becca start scratching her arms like she had a rash under her green and white baseball shirt, which turned into a distraught rubbing. She then appeared to brush herself off with a shiver as if she was covered in bugs or something. I watched her curiously: *What an odd girl.*

And then, together, we made the inexorable decision to enter Castle Shade.

Becca and I stepped through the white mist and into the front room of the castle. The air inside was cold and damp. I closed the door behind us and any sort of subtle ambient sound that remained from outside, whether it be the distant chirp of an insect or the rustling of the leaves on the ground, was cut off. Becca and I found ourselves surrounded by an unsettling silence inside the castle.

There was a soft drip that echoed from somewhere unseen, the sticky clicks from our shoes on the floor and a strange ringing in my ears that seemed to spike and then fade away once we entered.

The area we had entered into was dark, save for some outside light coming through from somewhere. It was an open room with not much to it that I could see; it reminded me of an empty hotel lobby...a creepy and decrepit one for sure, but that was the best comparison that came to mind. There was no furniture, no front desk (this was supposed to be a laboratory, right?).

"Where did you go when you were in here?" I asked Becca.

"Not any further than this really," she said. "I called out, but no one answered."

"What do you know of this place?" I asked.

She shook her head. Becca was even more clueless than I was. I proceeded to explain what information Mark and I had only found was vague at best. I explained that this was Castle Shade, home of the Shade Family Laboratory. Built well over one hundred years ago, it was supposedly on its fourth generation of Shade family owners.

"Well, it looks abandoned," Becca said. And as easy as it was to agree with her assessment, I refused to believe it. *Someone* led us here.

"Are they scientists?" Becca asked of the Shade family.

I didn't have an answer, but being a laboratory, I assumed there was science involved somehow. But what sort of active laboratory was *this* neglected and desolate?

Suddenly, something moved in my peripheral vision. I snapped my head to the right and my eyes were drawn to the floor in a shadowy corner of the room. Something had scurried into the blackness. I stared into the shadows, hoping my eyes would adjust just enough to see whatever it was.

"Did you see that?" I whispered.

I could feel Becca looking around now from behind me. I could feel her eyes scanning the room.

"I didn't see anything. What was it?" Becca responded.

The doll, I thought. I knew it was that damn baby doll creeping around in the shadows. It was *the doll* that led me here. This was his home after all. My nerves began to tingle again as I focused on the dark corner of the room. I cleared my mind and imagined the doll sitting on the floor, hidden by its shadowy blanket, watching us and laughing. It's laugh was disturbing with hints of mockery and a coltish malice.

Becca shrieked behind me, sending a high-pitched squeal bouncing off every wall in the room. I swung around and watched her hysterically brushing herself off. She screamed again and I grabbed her by the shoulders. I squeezed tightly, seizing her full attention.

"What is it?" I exclaimed.

She stopped and looked into my eyes; she was addled and appeared spooked as if she had experienced an illusory torment.

"They were on me..." she trembled.

I was confused. "*What* was on you?"

Shaken, Becca looked down at her body, seeing exactly what I saw - *nothing*. There was *nothing* on her. She caught her breath and tried to calm down. "Nothing," she shamefully confessed.

The front door of the castle creaked back open; I guess I hadn't closed it tight enough. Lines of sunlight from outside spread across the floor and illuminated the corner where the doll had deviously crept into. I glanced to the corner, expecting to see it sitting there in the daylight, but I was wrong. The corner was empty. There was no doll, no white eyes glaring, no menace lurking...this had become a game to him.

"Can we leave that door open?" Becca asked.

"Yeah," I said. I shook off the doll's presence and tried to focus on the room. I'd come all this way and discovered I wasn't the only one who had received letters. There had to be a logical explanation as to why the two of us were here. And now, it was time to find out.

There were four doorways along the walls of the room, not including the entrance. Two straight ahead and one on either side. Any one of those doors would lead us deeper into Castle Shade and any one of them could hold a clue, or even the answer, that would explain our being here.

"You check the door over there," I instructed Becca, pointing to the left side of the room. "I'll check this one." I started walking to the door opposite of her's, but stopped when I heard Becca say, "Uh, no."

"What?" I asked.

"Splitting up in a dark castle just doesn't seem like a smart idea," she said. "Haven't you seen *any* movies?"

She had a point, but this wasn't a movie. This was real life. A strange moment in real life, I'll admit, but the chances of some kind of demented castle freak with an axe lurking around every corner didn't seem all that plausible. That kind of thing didn't just happen in real life.

"We're sticking together," Becca said.

I reluctantly agreed. Not knowing who she was, I thought it would be best to avoid any kind of confrontation. Although, maybe she *wanted* us to stay together. Maybe she knew more than she was letting on.

"We'll go your way first," she said.

Becca then walked by me like she was taking charge. She walked to the door on the right side of the room and examined it before putting her hand on the chrome knob. I joined her side and encouraged her to continue. She turned the knob and pushed the door open.

The next room was just as dark. We walked in together, and I found myself immediately looking over my shoulder. Something felt very wrong. My eyes darted back and forth in the darkness, now fully expecting to see someone.

Emanating from the blackness, I heard someone breathing. It wasn't Becca and it definitely wasn't me. It was raspy, dry, and coming from in front of us.

"Hello?" I quietly called out. There was no answer, just the continuous breathing.

"Is someone in here?" Becca whispered to me. Her question came out with a quiver and she grabbed onto my sleeve.

"Who's there?" I called out a little louder. The elevated volume of my voice seemed to agitate the breather. It was louder now, husky and forced. Whoever, *whatever*, was in the room seemed distressed by us being there. Becca looked off to the side and I noticed her reach for something. She let go of my sleeve and grabbed a hold of something else. With a small click, she ignited a battery powered lantern. The bulb was dull and flickered as if it was in its last stretch of life, but there was enough of a glow coming from it to get a look at the room.

There was no one there and the breathing had come to an abrupt stop when the bulb lit up.

"It stopped," I said, confused.

"What stopped?" Becca asked.

"The breathing. You didn't hear it?"

"No..."

How could she have not heard it? It was the huskiest breathing I'd ever heard. *Someone* was just in here. *Someone* was messing with us. I stormed back out into the main room. Becca followed, still gripping the lantern, but now concerned. I could tell.

"Where are you going?" Becca yelled.

"I'm leaving," I said. "This is nonsense. I don't even know why I'm here. My wife needs me, and I have no actual business here."

I marched for the exit, enraged by my selfish decision to come here, and a loud, cracking *thud* stopped me in my tracks. Becca stopped chasing after me and we both stood still and silent in the castle lobby. At least Becca had heard *that*.

Thud. There it was again. It was coming from the door I had initially instructed Becca to go to.

"What is that?" she asked in a whisper.

Thud.

Someone was on the other side. I began to slowly walk to the door as the sounds continued. My nerves lit up again and my chest rattled. I didn't like being here anymore. And I only barely knew why I was here to begin with. My conscience told me to ignore the noises and just leave. Leave Becca, leave whoever was banging on the door. *Just. Leave.* But, my curiosity won the battle, and the smartest decision fizzled away into nothingness.

I was in front of the door, reaching for the chrome knob. Just as I was about to touch it, another *thud* made me jump back. I'd had enough. I grabbed the knob and turned it, swinging the door open towards me. Someone was on the other side and crashed to the floor in front of us. Becca gasped and I looked down at the stranger in disbelief.

The size and shape of the body led me to believe it was a man, but his hands and head were bound with some sort of material, hindering any visual that would identify him.

I continued to stand there, completely startled by the sight. The man grunted and groaned as if his mouth was gagged. Becca rushed to his side and sat the lantern down. She helped roll him onto his back and we both noticed the blood immediately; his leather jacket was covered in it.

"He's hurt!" Becca screamed. She frantically tried to unwrap his face and hands. "Sam, help me!"

I took a step toward them, but then felt an all too familiar presence. Dread flushed over me again, making me feel warm and dizzy. It could see me. It had its eyes on me once again. I looked up and saw it trying to hide in the shadows on the ceiling. But with white-hot eyes like that, it couldn't hide.

I watched the doll, firmly pressed against the ceiling. It continued to just stare at me, taunting me with quiet torment. Suddenly, it dropped, smacking the ground in front of me and sending a vibrating ringing deep into my ears as if a grenade had gone off. I covered my ears and winced. Keeping my eyes on the doll, which was motionless on its back, I waited for its next move. It wasn't done yet. All at once, both arms and both legs of the doll rotated and lifted itself off the ground. It's head turned unnaturally, once again resting its hollow gaze on me. Then it skittered across the floor like a manic spider, weaving back and forth and then quickly at me. I screamed and leapt out of the way.

"What?" Becca exclaimed. I looked at her as she helped the bloodied man to his feet. My heart was racing. The ringing in my ears faded back to silence and I scanned the floor around me. The doll was nowhere to be seen, and Becca seemed ignorant to it.

"Sam, help me," she begged, struggling to keep the man standing. I jogged over and helped unwrap the black gauze that concealed his head. When they came off, I saw the man's face. He spit out slobbery gauze that had been stuffed in his mouth and looked at me in relief.

"Thank you," the man said, catching his breath. He was tall and kept his black hair short and neatly buzzed. "I'm Symon," he introduced himself.

"Sam," I said.

"Becca."

I had noticed Becca hadn't included her last name this time when cautiously introducing herself. I wasn't sure if that meant she had learned from letting it slide with me, or possibly there was something about Symon that she didn't trust.

Symon looked around the lobby of Castle Shade as I unwrapped his hands. "Where are we?" he asked.

Becca and I shot each other a glance. This made three people now who didn't know either where they were, or why they were there.

"This place doesn't look familiar to you?" Becca asked. Symon shook his head.

I glanced down at the floor behind me where the doll had fallen, and it was nowhere to be found. I saw a flash of blood in my mind and turned right back to Symon. Blood covered his jacket.

"Are you hurt?" I asked him.

He looked down and acted surprised to see the blood. He shook his head again. "No, I don't think so."

"Who's blood is that?" Becca asked.

Symon grew even more confused. He appeared worried, as did Becca. I watched her body tense up, and she drew her arms in closer to her. She proceeded to scratch her arms again and then quickly brush them off. She must have had some sort of odd tic or something, as that was now the second time I witnessed this behavior from her. She shuddered and let out a weak gasp and then backed away from Symon, looking her own body over.

Symon noticed her behavior as well and asked, "Are you okay?"

Becca seemed to shiver and appeared disturbed. "They were all over me..." she said. "The worms..."

Symon looked at me for an answer, but I was just as lost. This was the first I'd heard her mention worms. From what I could see, there was nothing on her. Nor had there been. She must have been hallucinating.

That thought started to jostle my brain in various directions, and I had an unnerving thought: Had I been hallucinating? After all, Becca didn't see the baby doll drop from the ceiling and crawl across the floor. Only I did. Certainly that would have been noticed by someone else other than me. That is, unless it never happened to begin with.

I looked around the lobby, trying to take in the entire scope of Castle Shade and make sense of it all. It was an old abandoned castle, filled with creaks and cracks, cobwebs in every visible corner — was it haunted? My thought process mapped its way back to "Why was I here to begin with?" I didn't know anymore.

A doll moving on its own was impossible. It wasn't real. It couldn't be. Finally, I found myself thinking clearly for the first time since I arrived here and was flushed with shame and embarrassment. I had been tricked into coming and one of these two people before me were more than likely responsible.

"Why am I here?" I asked.

Becca, still clamping her arms to the sides of her body, looked at me. Symon looked at me too. They weren't going to answer my question, so I tried a different one.

"Why did you bring me here?"

Becca seemed confused. "I didn't bring you here. You came on your own. You came after me."

"I know that," I said. "But one of you must be behind this. And you were both here when I arrived, so, you obviously know something about this place. Who sent the letters?"

Neither Becca nor Symon answered. They chose to remain silent. I was growing more and more irritated with each passing second.

"How did you make that doll move?" I asked, now refusing to believe the trickery that I had fallen for.

Becca shook her head. "What? What doll?"

"Don't play stupid with me, Becca," I said. "The doll. The creepy doll with the white eyes. You used it to lure me here."

"I don't know what you're talking about!" Becca shouted, once again shaking the invisible worms off of her body. She squealed and backed away further as she brushed off her arms and then chest. She brushed her legs and shrieked again. I turned to Symon and he seemed to be in his head. Something was eating away at him inside. He started to hyperventilate and then said, "I killed them."

I couldn't comprehend what I was hearing and witnessing: *Had everyone gone mad?*

"Killed who?" I asked.

Symon brought attention to the blood on his jacket. "All of them. This is their blood. The caller was right..."

"Caller?" I asked.

"The guy who called me, blaming me and accusing me of the murders," Symon said. "He was so angry...so was I..."

"Who did you kill?" I asked.

That's where Symon drew a blank. His facial expression went from frantic to still. He looked at me and I could tell he either couldn't remember, or didn't want to say.

I turned back to Becca — she was gone. Only the lantern remained on the floor. I spun around desperately trying to see her in the lobby. I called out for her, but only my echo responded. I focused on the door that Symon had come out of. It was still open and blackness shrouded the inside of the unknown chambers. That was the only place she could have gone.

"What's in there?" I asked Symon, pointing at the room. He looked, only to humor me, but was too far gone in his own head. He shrugged. I picked up the lantern and made my way to the door. That's where I stopped, hesitating in the moment. I decided to call out for Becca once more before I would brave the unknown darkness.

"Becca?"

Nothing. I stuck the lantern in the room first and then followed it in. It's funny how a little bit of light can be comforting.

There was a dripping sound coming from somewhere in the room. It was louder than it had any right to be, but any other sound was absent.

"Becca?" I whispered this time. She didn't respond, but I had already expected her not to. Only the dripping sound was in here with me. I lifted the lantern up, shoulder level with me, and held it out as far as I could reach. I squinted, trying to see whatever I could, but it was impossible. The darkness overpowered the lantern's pathetic glow. I took a couple more steps in and tossed a quick look over my shoulder. The door was still open, but I couldn't see Symon. He was just out of view. My heartrate picked up again and I turned back to the ill-lit void that lay ahead. My breathing picked up, challenging the *drip, drip, drip* in the room for the loudest sound.

I stepped even further in. When I lifted my foot, a tacky residue snapped on the floor. I looked down, lowering the light to see what kind of sticky substance I was trudging through. That's when the light flickered inside the lantern and all went dark.

My heart stopped and my stomach twisted up in tight knots. A creaking noise erupted behind me, slow at first and then quickly became unafraid and thunderous. *The door!* I stood up and turned back to see the door closing fast. Someone was pulling it shut.

"Symon!" I screamed. The door closed and latched, permanently extinguishing the pale light from the lobby. In the pitch black, I rushed over to where I knew the door was. I felt around the wet walls and eventually found my way to the wooden door. I grabbed the knob but it wouldn't turn. It was jammed.

"Symon! Open the door!" I screamed again. There was no answer from Symon on the other side. There was no noise whatsoever.

I thought back to the blood that covered Symon and him claiming to have committed murders. It was him. *He* brought us here. He planned to kill us. But why? I'd never met him before in my life. But—

No. He was bound and gagged, trapped in a room. *This* room. Someone put him here too. Becca, maybe? She looked young and innocent, but that didn't mean anything. She could have been the mastermind behind this...whatever *this* was.

From my pocket, I pulled out my phone. I tried to call Kayla, but the signal was too weak. I tried texting her instead, but the text struggled to send, eventually coming back with a red *'failed to send'* notice beneath it. Technology wasn't all powerful after all. I shoved the phone back into my pocket and tried to concentrate. I took deep breaths. There had to be a way out. I still held the lantern and tried to smack it a few times and jiggle the knob.

"Come on…" I said to myself. "Work, dammit." I slapped the bottom where the batteries would go, and…

Light! The bulb flickered back on. The glow was weak but it was going to have to do. I needed to make full use of it before it decided to shut off on me again. I held it up to the doorknob and tried to turn it again, but it was useless. I knocked on the door viciously with my free hand.

"Symon! Becca! Someone open the door!" I shouted. I put my ear to the door and tried to listen for anyone out in the lobby. And not surprising at all, it was quiet. I faced the darkness again and took some cautious steps further. I didn't know how big the room was, or even if there were any other…

Doors! That's it. There had to be another door. I moved to the closest wall and held the lantern up as close as I could to get the weak light to work with me. I started to walk the perimeter of the room, snapping through the sticky substance on the floor, praying I'd find another way out. I was over Castle Shade.

Drip, drip, drip...

That constant sound seemed to get louder by the minute. Was it a leaking pipe? Moisture from the walls? Something that spilled and was now dripping from a table?

I heard something move; the first sound in the room other than the drip and myself.

"Becca?" I called out, hopeful that it was her.

The noise continued. It was hard to make out, but seemed like something shuffling about. It went from one side of the room to the other fairly quickly and then stopped. The dark was now disorienting, and I didn't know which direction was which. But now I knew that someone, or something, was in the room with me.

"She screamed," a small, haunting voice whispered from the darkness. I'd heard it before and I knew exactly who it was.

The doll.

"Where are you?" I grit my teeth, becoming angry once again by the malefic object. It was haunting me, trying to frighten and unravel me. *What did it want?*

I lost my patience. "Where are you!" I screamed. Two white eyes immediately lit up across the room - a shrill cry accompanied it. The eyes pulsated with a searing whir, loud enough to split my head open. I closed my eyes and slapped my hands over my ears, dropping the lantern. I couldn't even hear it shatter on the ground over the terrible sound the doll was emitting.

"Stop it!" I screamed.

It complied. There was silence once again. The whirring sound had stopped, as did the terrible shriek. I opened my eyes to the pitch black room. The white eyes were gone and the slow dripping sound faded back in.

I could hear my heart beating, thumping wickedly just beneath my ribs. The dark was starting to strain my nerves. I felt uncomfortable and restless, like I was stuck in a dream that I couldn't awake from. It reminded me of a recurring dream I had when I was younger:

All the lights in my house were off. No matter what I did, I couldn't find a lightswitch. Whenever I felt like I had found one, my legs went heavy, like they were made of concrete, preventing me from getting too close. There were screams in the distance outside that hoisted my fear, making me cry and quake with panic. There was laughter from just outside the windows - something was always watching me, mocking me. It celebrated my fear. Through the tattered, blowing curtains against the window, I could only make out two, small egg-shaped eyes, glowing white hot outside. A cackling laugh vented from its emotionless and lifeless porcelain mein.

In the dark room within the stone walls of Castle Shade, I could feel the doll's presence again. It was like the dream I'd had since childhood had come to life. The doll was there and the darkness swallowed everything. I had no light, no way out -

My phone, I thought. How had I not thought of it before. I had a flashlight on my phone - I didn't need the lantern. I fumbled in my pocket and pulled out my phone. The screen lit up, and

the time stared me in the face. It was after 7pm.
I'd been here all day. I held down the button on
the screen that ignited the light on the
opposite side. I squinted as my eyes absorbed
the most vivid light they'd endured since
entering the castle.

The slow drip continued and I shined my
light around the room. It was larger than I
thought it would be, stretching longer than it
was in width. There were more doors. Two of
them actually. Both were side by side at the far
end. I aimed the light at the ceiling, looking for
the drip, but failed to observe any pipes. The
floor was sticky, so I aimed the light down at
my feet next.

There was a dark red substance coating the
stone floor. It wasn't until I saw the substance
that I felt like I could smell it. It smelled ripe,
rusty...a shiver crept through my bones when I
jumped to the assumption that the mysterious
substance could be blood. I shook off the
quivering chill and looked ahead again, toward
the two doors on the other side of the room.
The one on the right seemed to be open and
leading into yet another dark room. The one to

the left was blocked by a wooden door framed by metal plating.

I took my time as I approached the doors. The slapping sound beneath my shoes was starting to drive me crazy. I didn't like the thought of old blood covering the floor, so I held onto hope that it wasn't. That hope was minimal, however. I took a deep breath and exhaled slowly as I now stood before the two doorways.

Drip, drip.

It was louder now, like I should have been able to see what it was. The murky room that loitered to the right of me was filled with a cold and barren secret; a strange feeling slithered just beneath my skin. Instinct told me not to reveal the secret, but as the dripping sound started to gouge deeper into my conscience, I had to see for myself where it was originating from.

I stepped in the room's direction, holding the light down by my side momentarily, building up the self-confidence I needed to just look. I was poised and ready now. A quick flash of unease and fear stung my body like a strike of lightning and I lifted my light.

Hanging in front of me, in the shallowest part of the dark room, was the lower half of a woman's body. It gently swayed back and forth, creaking, with blood dripping from her shadowy top half and pittering into a red puddle beneath her. The blood webbed out from the puddle into small rivers that traveled in the cracks of the stone floor.

I gasped and stumbled backwards, crunching something beneath my shoes. I looked down, lifted my foot, and saw a pair of sunglasses completely shattered. As I looked at the bent white frames splintered across the floor at my feet, I noticed the faded image of the Looney Tunes logo. I knew who those sunglasses belonged to...

I aimed the light back up at the swaying corpse in the dark room. She was dressed in black jogging pants, running shoes, and I could tell she was wearing a blue shirt. I swallowed hard as my body began to shudder. My heart was beating fast and I felt flushed and light-headed. I hesitated briefly before training the light on the top half of her.

She was almost unrecognizable. With a thick noose wrapped around her neck, her skin looked bleached, her lips were cracked, peeling and curled in a disturbingly unnatural way. Her eyes were ajar, cloudy and void of all life.

It was Madison, Kayla's missing sister, who hung before me.

PART TWO
OF A MAD BRAIN

"*She screamed! She screamed! She screamed!*" the little voice viciously repeated.

"Shut up!" I screamed back at it, covering my ears and clamping my eyes shut. "Just shut up!" My teeth grinded against one another, top jaw to bottom.

"*She screamed,*" the voice said again, calmer this time and allowing the words to echo through the vast room I had collapsed in. My phone, on the floor beside me, kept Madison's legs in view of the light. She continued to sway, blood dripping down, and the rope that suspended her creaked back and forth from a hook on the ceiling.

She screamed, I thought. She screamed when the picture fell from above Kayla's vanity. It cracked, separating Madison from us. Separating the dead from the living. She screamed - *she died* - at that very moment.

What was this place? Why was I here? Kayla needed to know what happened; where her sister was. I picked up my phone and tried to call my wife. The signal was dead. I was getting nothing. Now, a red flicker at the top of the screen indicated the battery was dangerously low.

I held the light out again and watched my sister-in-law dangle from the ceiling, mostly embedded in sinister shadows.

Why was she here? Why the *hell* was she here? A million different thoughts and scenarios ravaged my mind, but none of them connected into a single, plausible idea. I couldn't imagine any logical reason why

Madison would be in the same castle as I was. Not to mention Becca and Symon...

"I killed them," I recalled Symon admitting. This was his doing. This was his fault! He was the reason Madison was dead! He killed her! He killed...*them*...

There were more. There had to be more bodies in Castle Shade. The place was massive; God only knew what other horrors were concealed within its walls. A cold gust encircled me, and I turned my attention to the other door. It was open now; I didn't recall seeing it open before. The cold gust came from the other side of that door. I stood up and aimed my light in that direction. I crept toward it and peered in. There was a long, dark hallway with a soft orange glow at the end of it.

I aimed my light down the hall, but it only allowed me to see so much. I waited, afraid to step foot into the hall. But the constant to and fro creaking from the rope kept half of my attention on Madison. I felt sick. This was a woman who was the maid of honor at my wedding. The aunt of my son. The life of every family gathering. A beautiful soul who met a gruesome end. The *why* was nagging me more than anything though. Why was Madison dead...*here*.

Suddenly, a guttural, blood-curdling scream erupted from down the hall. It shattered me, and instinct took over. I dashed for the doorway but stopped abruptly. I hesitated - did I really want to see? Did I really need to know?

The scream exploded again, echoing down the hall and blasting my ears. It was a woman's scream. *Becca?* I wondered.

One more explosive scream from her was followed by a grim, "Help me!" I rushed into the hall and ran as fast as I could toward the screaming.

"Hold on!" I yelled back, hoping that Becca, or whoever it was, would know help was coming. She continued to scream; it sounded like she was being murdered. The screams intensified as I inched ever closer. The orange glow was getting brighter, now dancing with shadows on the walls. I made it to the end of the hallway and turned the only corner there was.

I emptied out into a large room, filled with burning candles. They were on the dusty dinner table that sat in the middle of the room. They hung from mounts on the walls, dangled from a chandelier above the table. The room was old; spiderwebs fluttered everywhere, and dirty white sheets kept other furniture in the room unseen. Along the far wall was a large stained glass window. Shadowy tree branches danced on the other side of it as rain began its pitter-patter against it.

I heard a rumble of thunder outside, followed by a soft flash of lightning. It lit up the stained glass window, casting the room briefly in a rainbow of colors. Once the room settled back into darkness, with the soft orange glow of the candles being my only light, I heard the scream again. It was louder, more fervent than before. She wasn't in this room. To the left of the window, tucked inside of the blackened corner, was another dim doorway. That had to be where she was.

I ran through the room and into the next dark corridor. I could still hear her screaming; it sounded close. I ran, passing open doors on

my left that sunk back deep into inky unknown
chambers.

Her scream was thunderous now, just as
roaring as the actual thunder that started to
crash and boom outside like a maniacal
drummer. Until the lighting viciously sparked,
I was dumb to the fact that a dozen windows
paneled the wall to my right. The unexpected,
seizure-inducing lightshow knocked me to the
floor. I gathered my strength and heard the
scream again. She was just up ahead.

I raced down the rest of the hallway, spilling
out into another room similar to the
candle-filled one, only this one was without a
single burning wick. I held up my light and
there she was.

Becca stood in the middle of the room,
screaming and shaking violently, like she was
experiencing a seizure of her own. She
viciously swept her legs with her hands and
then brushed her arms, her hair - she clawed at
her face sending blood trickling down her neck
and under the collar of her shirt.

"Becca!" I shouted as I rushed to her side.
Trying to keep the light on her, I put a hand on

her shoulder. "What's wrong?! What's happening?!"

"Get them off me! Get them off!" she screamed almost inaudibly. I looked her up and down, shining my light from her head to her legs. There was *nothing* on her. I didn't know what to do. I looked at her bloody face; I was speechless and deeply disturbed.

"Sam!" Becca wailed with wild emotion. "Help me!"

I was unclear as to what to do. Ultimately, her hysteria was convincing enough. Even though I knew there was nothing on her, I feigned helping. I brushed off her legs and then her back. I swatted at nothing after nothing, pretending to clear her shoulders from the non-existent force that tormented her.

Finally, she dropped to her knees, sobbing, but much more tranquil. I caught my breath from the sudden chaos and knelt down beside her. Her eyes were red and her face was damp from the tears. She wheezed as she caught her own breath and then looked at me with irritated eyes.

A look of horror grew upon her. Her green eyes widened, and she let out a loud gasp before covering her face with her hands. Only her eyes remained visible, warily gazing upon me from just above her fingertips.

"What?" I asked.

Shakily, she stood to her feet and started to back away from me, as if *I* now frightened *her*.

"What's wrong?" I asked again.

"They're on you now..." she whispered.

"No," I said, shaking my head. There had been nothing on Becca to begin with, therefore, there was nothing on me. She was losing her mind; she was unhinged. I opened my arms out wide to display my whole self. "No, Becca. There's nothing on me. There was nothing on you, either."

Keeping one hand covering her quivering mouth, she used her other one to point at me. Her finger, trembling almost uncontrollably, dipped down to bring attention to my lower half. Once again, to humor her, I looked down and aimed my light.

There, I saw a mound - an undulating mass - of slick, black worms that I stood inside of.

They squelched and squirmed all around my legs, up just past my knees, emitting hundreds of stifled moans between the thousands of them. I screamed and leapt out of the pile as fast as I could, stumbling to the corner and rapidly shaking them off my legs. I could hear them slap as they hit the floor, but hidden by the room's darkness, I couldn't tell where they were landing.

I lifted my light and saw Becca standing across the room, continuing to cover her mouth. Her eyes darted back and forth in a frenzy as the door behind her slowly creaked open. I tried to see who was opening it, so I shifted to the right just enough to aim my light behind her. The light gleamed off of something metallic, which rose up through the darkness. I squinted, just barely seeing the face of Symon. The gleaming reflection was over his head before I had time to comprehend what it was.

It was an axe.

"Becca, move!" I screamed. But it was too late. Symon swung the axe down. He buried it into the center of Becca's back, sending blood streaming out of her like an explosion of red ribbons.

I was immediately struck with overpowering disbelief. Becca's body fell face first to the ground with the axe planted firmly in her. Symon stumbled backwards and stopped against the wall. His wide eyes and gaping jaw were reminiscent of how I felt. *What had he done?*

I rushed over to Becca as soon as I regained my composure and rolled her onto her side; the weight of the axe made it more difficult to move her. I aimed the light on her and her eyes were shut and she was soaked in crimson.

"What have you done?" I growled, looking up to Symon. "Why did you kill her?"

Symon just looked at me with dead eyes. He seemed confused, or clueless as to what had just happened.

"Where did you get the axe?" I asked.

He lazily pointed behind him, referring to the room he had emerged from. He took a step toward Becca's body and I, but I was quick to my feet. I put my arm out to stop him.

"Don't you dare come any closer," I said. Symon stopped moving. He was a cold-blooded killer. He took Becca's life before my very eyes, as well as the other's he had alluded to earlier. Possibly even Madison's.

"Did you kill Madison?" I asked.

He continued to just stare at me.

"That woman back there!" I shouted, pointing back in the other direction. "You were in the room with her! You killed her!"

Symon became even more confused. He didn't appear to have any idea what I was talking about, so his response didn't add up:

"Yes," he said. "I killed her. I killed them all..."

"Who? Who else did you kill?"

Symon didn't have an answer. He refused to say anything else. I knelt back down to Becca's side, ignorantly believing there was something I could do for her. I had never seen a dead body before in my lifetime, and now in a matter of minutes, I found myself a witness to two grisly scenes of murder.

I caressed Becca's hair for a moment, mournful for her and her family. Then, as my fingers grazed the skin of her forehead, her eyes shot open.

The beautiful green eyes she once possessed were gone, both now replaced with pulsating, white-hot radiance. The freakish knell that had ceaselessly partnered with the glow was back with ferocity. I covered my ears and stumbled back, falling into the anomalous mass of black worms. They all cried out upon my touch, sounding like tragic souls trapped in hell, imploring to be saved.

I leapt back up to my feet and heard the distant cackle of the baby doll. It bounced through the empty hallways of Castle Shade and into the room with us. It was a scornful beast, the doll, relishing every moment of maelstrom I experienced.

Symon approached me just as a loud blast of thunder exploded outside and a series of violent lightning strikes lit up the room. The doll's laughter vanished within the booming thunder and when I shot a glance at Becca, her eyes were closed again. I looked down at the mass of writhing worms, but they too were gone.

Symon's hand appeared before me in a helpful manner. I chose not to accept it and stood to my feet on my own. I faced him. "What are you doing to me?" I asked. "What have you done? Why am I here? Why--"

The questions I had for him were endless, but a migraine suddenly attacked my brain, preventing me from continuing. I knelt back down, trying to wish the pain away, and Symon crouched down by my side.

"Listen, something's going on here," he said. "I didn't do anything. I didn't mean to..."

I looked up at him, wondering how he was going to talk himself out of the murder I just watched him commit. But, somehow, his next words...I knew were coming.

"I wasn't myself," he said. "I don't know what's wrong with me. I didn't realize what I was doing until it was done. I panicked."

"Panicked?" I asked. "You killed her. Without reason. She was losing her mind when you—"

"Exactly," Symon uttered, "she was crazy. Why? What was she freaking out about?"

I gawked at Symon, wondering why someone freaking out would warrant a vicious demise. "Worms," I said. "She was covered in worms."

"Worms?" Symon asked. "There was nothing on her."

"That's because I helped her get them off. They were on me after that. Right there," I said, pointing to where the mound of black worms had been. Symon looked to where I was pointing the light.

"Where?" he asked.

"They're gone now," I said.

"You saw them?"

"Yes. They were all over me. They were...screaming."

Symon seemed mystified by what I was saying. "There was nothing in here, Sam. There were no worms."

As I stood to my feet once again, the blue glow of lightning winked through the few small windows on the wall and I was rattled by the crash of thunder that followed. I could hear the rain pounding the side of the castle outside, as well as the hollering of a strong wind.

Symon didn't see the worms. He didn't see them on Becca and he didn't see them on me. But, did he hear the baby doll?

"What about the laughter?" I asked. "From the baby doll."

"The what?" he asked. He genuinely seemed perplexed.

"The doll. The doll that's been mocking me. It's been laughing at me ever since we got here. It was in my car. It was on the book at the—"

"Stop talking," Symon abruptly said, preventing my mounting distress from piquing. He put his finger up to his lips as an extra measure to keep me silent. I did as he said and listened.

"Do you hear that?" Symon asked.

I didn't hear anything aside from the unholy storm raging outside. But, Symon did. He was hearing something that I wasn't. He snapped his head to the right, and then to the left. Whatever he heard was either getting closer or was already there. *I* still didn't hear anything.

"What is it?" I whispered.

He was quick to hush me once again and then began to slowly step backwards. He started to mumble inaudible words that sounded as if he were praying.

"Symon?"

He swung himself around in a flash, looking into the shadows behind him. He screamed, spurting out a series of expletives and then spun back around and rushed toward me. "Run!"

I froze as he raced by me, trying to grab my arm as he did so. He couldn't get a grip on my sleeve, so he kept running. What the *hell* was going on?

"Sam! Run!" he screamed at me again. I turned to see him disappearing into the corridor. I turned back to the shadows that frightened him, wanting to see what he had seen. As I focused my eyes on the darkness, trying to make out anything I could, lightning lit up the room again. Within the sharp surges of blue light, I saw nothing but an empty corner in which he ran from. I wondered...

What if Symon had seen apparitions of his victims. Of all the people he had murdered. Becca, Madison—*all* of the others. What if they were in the room provoking him, as the doll was doing to me. What if Castle Shade was...*of course!*

It is a house that haunts you with its ghosts; *your* ghosts.

Symon was being haunted by his murdered victims. I was being stalked by the doll. Becca had succumbed to a fear of worms...

Come see the ghosts for yourself.

We'd all been lured here by our fears, our curiosities. Someone was—

—I felt the touch of a cold hand on the back of my neck. Its skin was rough and dry and felt like ice. Every single hair on my body stood on end as if they were all alerted to an imminent threat and I entered a state of paralysis. It was one of Symon's victims.

I felt a cold, rotten breath breathing by my ear. The craggy inhaling and exhaling seemed to spit clotted substances onto my neck and shoulders. I combatively broke free from the wraith's grip and bounded into the hallway where Symon had vanished.

I huffed as I ran down the narrow corridor, the light from my phone brandishing here and there on the floor and walls. Lightning continued to throb unapologetically through the windows to my left. Thunder clapped and exploded seconds later, tossing me like a ragdoll into one of the blackened rooms to my right. I hit the floor hard. The impact knocked the wind out of me and the phone from my hand. It spun through the air and hit something, causing the light to fatally dispel.

"No..." I stammered. That light was my salvation. In this spectral dwelling we were trapped in, that light was imperative to my solace, my survival.

I stood up in the room, watching the lightning continue to spark out in the hallway. The room I was in was cold and musty. I looked around, using the sudden charges of lightning to take in as much of the room as I could. It was like putting together a mental puzzle using only flashes of the pieces to create the entire picture. But, I had a decent idea of the layout.

The room was no bigger than a storage closet. There was a table along the wall with an old portrait of a man hanging on the wall above it; probably an important member of the Shade family.

There was another door as well. I could see a subdued greenish light creeping out from underneath it. I approached the door and felt for the knob. As my hand gripped the cold metal of the doorknob, another series of lightning flashes illuminated the room again. There was a dusty plaque on the wall with the words Subject One engraved on it.

My mind began to race with every morbid possibility of what was behind the door. I tried to turn the knob, but it didn't move. It was like it was only for show. I looked the door up and down and between the blue flashes, I saw the sides and top of the door were sealed, affixed to the door frame from the outside with gnarled solder. No one was meant to get in or out. It gave me the impression that it was a makeshift jail cell of some sort, haphazardly created years, maybe decades, earlier.

However, the door itself was still made of aged, average wood. And there was an axe just down the hall. If I was going to find out the truth behind Castle Shade, and who brought me here, I needed to see what was hidden behind the door.

Back down the hallway, in the room where Becca's bloody body lay, I gripped the handle of the axe. With the blade still embedded into her back, I couldn't just pull it out with ease. I tugged lightly at first, pulling her body along as I did so. I then put my foot down on her lower back and yanked harder. The blade ripped out with a *crunch* and sent me stumbling backward. I gained my composure and fought back the vomit that had foregathered in my throat. A deep breath later, I retreated back down the hallway.

I stood before the door labeled Subject One. The numerous other rooms in the hall I passed looked identical; I assumed the only difference would be the engraving on the door plaques; Subject Two, Three, and so on. Having sealed rooms with subjects was the first sign I'd seen of Castle Shade living up to the science laboratory it was classified as.

But who, or *what*, were the subjects?

I gripped the axe handle with both hands, hoping my sweaty palms didn't hinder my attempts at bashing the door in. I wound up and used every ounce of strength in my body to slam the blade into the door. It chipped and cracked loudly. I did it again, creating another gash in the door. The soft green light now beamed out from the two vertical lacerations, accentuating the floating dust in the room I stood in.

I slammed the axe into the door again and again. The cluster of splintered cuts I had made had created a large weak spot in the wood. I leaned the axe against the wall and kicked the rest of the door in, releasing an assault on my senses; a terrible odor gushed out of the cell as did countless roaches. They skittered around my feet and out into the depths of the castle. I held my shirt over my nose and entered the green-glowing room.

It didn't take long for me to find the source of the profound fetor. The skeletal remains of a human lay in the middle of the cell. The bones were clean of any skin or organs and even appeared cracked and brittle; they looked like they'd been there for decades. Spiders webbed through the eye sockets, mouth, and created a twisted network of silky mesh throughout the rib cage.

I looked up from the bones to a dirty window on the wall in which the green light was stemming from behind. I walked around the bones and to the window. It was coated by a thick layer of dust and grime. Dead bugs were bonded into the filth, as were some scarce live ones. I used my hand to wipe away a portion of the accumulated dirt. The green light now shined through the clearing with more intensity, making me squint at first. I leaned closer, covering my nose once again in hopes of not inhaling any more of the wretched odor and tainted dust.

Through the clean swipe I had made, I could see a laboratory; sterile and modern - the complete contrast of my experience with the rest of Castle Shade. Roused, yet genuinely unclear, I scoured my only view of the lab with analytical eyes. There were steel tables, stools and chairs, computers, test tubes, mounds of files and paperwork as well as numerous other windows like the one I was looking through (I counted at least six bordering the room). The green glow in the lab was curious, but paled as dread for my obscure conundrum swelled.

My heart began to pound uncontrollably; fear invaded every ounce of me. Something was off. Even in this surreal nightmare, I found myself anticipating a novel danger. And when I heard the squishy footsteps approaching behind me, I froze. The footsteps came to a stop and a man's voice boorishly asked, "Who are you?"

I turned around as the lightning raged and the thunder cracked. A man, about my height, stood silhouetted in the doorway of the cell. I couldn't make out any of his features until the strobing lightning relaxed. The beaming green light from inside the laboratory now gave me a full picture of him.

He was tall and lanky. His receding hairline gave way to a wrinkled forehead in which two bushy eyebrows protected his two tired eyes. He wore a long black trench coat that was closed like a curtain around him and secured by a belt. The man was soaked from head to toe, presumably having just entered the castle from the relentless storm.

"Who are you?" he repeated louder. I couldn't tell if he was concerned by my presence, or if he saw me as a trespasser on a property that I didn't belong on.

"Sam," I replied.

The man's leer was calculating; curious, yet cautious. Whether or not he was on the offensive or the defensive, his mannerisms made it clear he didn't want to act first. A wrong move for him would have undetermined consequences. I was playing defense and wasn't about to let my guard down.

The man glanced down to his right where I had leaned the axe.

"Don't," I commanded, adding volume to my voice. The man just looked back at me.

"Is that yours?" he asked.

"Yes," I said. "See the blood on it? I won't hesitate to use it on you either."

The man smirked. "How would you even grab it?" he arrogantly asked. "If you took one step in my direction, I'd pick it up and bury that bloody blade into your skull faster than a cat on a mouse."

I conceded that as a real possibility, so I decided to rout the aggressive angle and try a more decorous one. I watched the rain water drip from his coat, pooling on the floor around his shoes. It was eerily reminiscent of the blood dripping and pooling beneath Madison's body. The green glow gave him an otherworldly appearance and I fought away the creeping thoughts that the doll was behind this entire charade. I didn't know how, or why, he would conduct such a tactic, but in Castle Shade it wouldn't have been the strangest event to occur.

"Who are you?" I asked calmly. "I told you my name."

The man finally seemed to relax, mirroring my change in tone. He wiped the dripping water from his brow and said, "Hektor."

"What brings you here, Hektor?"

He hesitated for a moment and then reached into his coat pocket. My guard was up once more as he extracted a white envelope. It was folded over twice and crinkled in his grip as he opened it. Hektor pulled out a note and an accompanying black and white photo of what I assumed to be the castle. He had been lured here too; I should have known.

"Was that your car out there across the bridge?" Hektor asked. I nodded. "And the bike?"

"That was Becca's..." I trailed off, remembering the sudden crunch of the axe blade into her spine.

"Where's Becca?" Hektor asked, probably noticing the discomfort in my face when I uttered her name.

I pointed in the direction of the room where her corpse lay. Hektor glanced back down to the axe and then lifted an eye at me. "Did you..."

"No," I said.

"But you threatened me with it. There's a lot of blood on it, Sam."

"It wasn't me," I insisted. "It was Symon."

Hektor looked baffled, but I understood why. He had just arrived and so much had already happened. So much...*blood*...

"The tall man in the leather coat?" Hektor asked, blindsiding me with that knowledge.

"Yes. Did you see him?"

Hektor nodded. "He's dead. He's impaled on what's left of the bridge outside."

I could only imagine the look of momentous shock on my face. Hektor displayed brief sympathy and then focused his attention on the green laboratory behind me. He stepped closer, focusing intently on the lab. He pointed at it and smirked as he sidled up next to me. "That used to be my lab," he said.

Wait, what? I couldn't believe what I had just heard. *His* lab? Was this *his* Castle? I looked at the bones on the floor that Hektor had so insouciantly walked around.

"You live here?" I asked.

Hektor shook his head. "No. I used to work for the Shade family. It's been years since I've set foot in the place." Hektor looked down at the bones and a glimmer of concern spread across his face. "I didn't think this was all still going on..." he ominously whispered to himself.

"Wh-what's going on?" I asked.

Hektor looked me in the eyes. His were filled with fear, worry — unease. They appeared glassy and his lips quivered. "I signed away my rights to speak of it," he said before restlessly looking around. He then whispered, "The consequences would be grim, pitiless."

"What are you talking about? Hektor, what is this place?"

"I'm sorry," Hektor whimpered. He reached into his coat pocket, the same one he had removed the envelope from, and pulled out a small snub nosed revolver.

I panicked. He was going to kill me. I knew I had seen too much. I didn't *want* to see any of it. I didn't *want* to ever be here in the first place. "Just let me go," I begged.

"I'm sorry," he repeated, detached, yet doleful. "I'm sorry you were chosen." Hektor placed the barrel of the revolver to his temple and pulled the trigger. The *boom* rang violently in my ears as Hektor plummeted to the floor. I roared in bewilderment and covered my ears before retreating back into the hallway. Again, the thunder rocked the foundation of Castle Shade and the lightning electrified my path back down to the room where Madison's body hung. I crashed through the room, refusing to look at her body again, and to the door which had shut on me earlier. It was open now, presumably from Hektor's entrance. I dashed

through and back into the lobby of Castle
Shade.

The wind roared outside, blowing horizontal
rain in through the open entrance I'd originally
come in from. Water rushed across the floor as
shredded pieces of leaves swirled into the
lobby. The door creaked fervently on its hinges,
rattling against the hard winds. Thunder and
lightning continued to pummel the outdoors. I
scurried through the lobby, positioning myself
a safe distance from the brutal weather, but
also trying to see out the open door.

It was like a hurricane outside. Tree's were
bending, leaves and debris galloped across the
ground and the downpour made it near
impossible to see much else. I couldn't see the
bridge, my car...

The bridge. Symon had tried to make an
escape. Hektor saw him impaled on what was
left of the bridge. What was left of it? Had the
bridge been destroyed? *How? Why?*

Just then, I saw the shape of a man
materialize in the rain outside. He just stood
there, belabored by the storm. Someone else
was here. *A friend? Foe?*

"Hello?" I called out to him. He didn't move. For a moment, I thought I was just seeing things or maybe even just the outline of a displaced tree or some other natural object. That is, until his arm moved, revealing the shadowy, unmistakable outline of an axe.

I froze. Fear engulfed me once more as the shadowy figure began to walk toward me. I swallowed hard and took a few steps backward. The figure crossed the threshold and into the lobby, stomping down on the old wooden floor. The rainwater sloshed beneath his soles and blood dripped from his dark clothing, mixing with the rain to create waves of red water on the floor.

It was Symon. He stood in the lobby, facing me with lunacy in his eyes. He gripped the axe handle tightly with one hand and then with both. I could see the impalation Hektor had mentioned. A wooden shard from the bridge stuck into his shoulder and protruded out the other side. Blood actively poured from his wounds. Symon cracked his neck to the side and continued walking toward me with a menacing resolve.

I backed up further until my back hit the wall. This couldn't be real. There was no way. Symon was dead. Symon was...a ghost?

Come see the ghosts for yourself.

Symon expelled a repulsive gurgling sound and raised the axe over his head.

"Symon, don't!" I screamed. He charged me, swinging the axe down and releasing an appalling cry as he did so. The steel blade slammed the wooden wall behind me as I quickly dove out of the way. He tore the blade from the wall and savagely swung it around at me. I again noticed the two other doors along the wall that I'd seen when I first entered the castle. I raced to them, slipping on the wet floor but keeping my balance. Symon unnaturally shrieked again as he chased me to the doors. He had a better grip on the axe now. He swung with an elevated ruthlessness, but missed again. The metal blade smacked the floor, giving me enough time to reach the doors. The first one I tried to open worked and I slipped in, pulling it shut behind me. In yet another dark room, I could hear a chain lock jangling on the door. I felt for it and when it touched my fingers, I latched it and stepped away from the door as Symon angrily roared on the other side. I took two steps backwards and lost my balance. I tumbled down a stairwell in the pitch black, not knowing where I was falling to or how far down it was. I hit my head against the wall, knocked my knee and sliced my arm on the way down.

I finally hit the ground with a body-rattling thud. The floor was cold, wet and felt rough like unfinished pavement. My head was pounding and for sure bleeding. I struggled to my feet, my knees shaking weakly as I did.

As I caught my breath, I heard a faint whisper in the blackness. It was soft and inaudible at first. I heard it again. It seemed to be closer now. I chose not to call out to it. Holding my ground, I desperately tried to see something - *anything* - in the darkness.

"*You'll scream,*" it said in a whispering hiss. It was the doll. Two white ovals ignited before me, eye-level with mine. They burned white hot and the dreadful ringing sound returned. I cringed and held my head, but the throbbing seemed to pump more and more blood from the gash on my temple. I grew weak, woozy.

"*Scream!*" the doll commanded, dropping its whisper in favor of a deeper, more vile voice. It grabbed my arm and viciously tugged.

"Shut up! Shut up!" I screamed back. Right then, there was light. Small lights on the ceiling flickered on one by one, displaying the path in front of me; a long tunnel that reminded me of a mineshaft or a part of some underground catacombs. The kicker was, *no one* stood in front of me now. With the lights now on, the doll was gone. Only the cold silence and enigma of what skulked in the tunnel ahead of me remained.

I looked back up the rocky stairwell behind me and at the door I had bolted shut. All was quiet there too; Symon had halted his barbaric onslaught, but I didn't know for how long. I wasn't safe anywhere. I turned back to face the extended tunnel ahead and began to amble through it.

Water dripped from the low ceiling, plopping down into puddles on the floor. I walked through cold spots and areas with unexplained mugginess. The whole time I felt like I was being watched, or hunted. Even the walls appeared to breathe, bubbling up and exhaling rotten air. I kept my focus and picked up speed. My footsteps echoed through the shaft as did my wheezing. I couldn't reach the end of the hallway fast enough and now I felt like I was being pursued quickly. I tossed my head over my shoulder for only a brief moment and saw Symon gaining on me, the axe gripped tightly in his hands.

"No!" I screamed. I now ran like I was in a marathon. Symon was getting closer. No matter how fast I tried to run, he was faster. There was another tunnel up ahead and I veered right, seeing a half open door at the end of the next stretch. I charged even faster now, optimistic that the room ahead would provide me some sort of asylum.

I could feel Symon breathing right down my neck - he was closing in. I was running so fast that the veins in my neck felt like they would burst at any moment. They began to pulsate with pain, filling with blood and then flattening back out. It felt wrong - it felt like

my veins had lives of their own and were
deliberately inflicting the nauseating torment
on me. I grit my teeth and reached up for my
neck, placing my palm over the palpitating
organs.

They were covered by a viscid substance and
screamed like hell when I touched them. I
pulled my hand back to see it covered by the
black, heinous worms. I panicked and heaved
my entire body forward in an attempt to detach
them from my skin. I shook like a dog and
watched them splat against the wet stone walls
and drown in the endless puddles that littered
the floor. I looked back and was met by the
raging unpigmented eyes of the doll looming
over me. It reached its cracked hands toward
me and I thrashed my arms at it, knocking it to
the ground. It was then trampled over by
Symon. My eyes widened as he raised the axe
above his head; my death was inescapable. I
crashed through the half open door and
collapsed into a bright room. I had been so
relentlessly stalked by the worms, the doll and
Symon, that I forgot I had still been running

the whole time. I stood to my feet, shaky and completely enervated.

The room was cold. I could hear the soft hum of an air conditioner coming from somewhere, but that was the only sound. That and a few sporadic, yet soft computerized beeps, like a serene hospital room. I studied my new surroundings: It was another laboratory; another pristine, sterile one. The computers were modern, the equipment looked complex. A bubbling sound grabbed my attention and I turned around. By the open door, where I had come in, was a steel table with test tubes, microscopes, a Centrifuge and hooks along the wall with safety goggles and lab coats hanging from them.

A couple of electrical devices that shot a stable jolt of electricity from one to the other sat on a smaller table next to it. It looked like a tightrope made of a controlled blue and green lightning bolt. My first thought was that this place resembled Dr. Frankenstein's laboratory. It was a room straight out of old horror fiction with its equipment, mood and mystery — and buried deep in the pits of a dilapidated castle, it could have *only* been the creation of a mad scientist.

Further to my left was a clear plastic tub that was filled with a limpid solution. I approached it and saw that, soaking in the solution, was some sort of black ribbon. Upon closer look, the ribbon was textured as only medical gauze would be. *Black gauze — why did that look familiar?* I wondered and then it hit me. Symon's face was wrapped in identical gauze when he came out of the room.

What was that solution it was in? I leaned closer to the tub and felt my heart rate pick up almost instantly. I felt nervous, afraid...afraid of the doll! I swung around, expecting to see the doll glaring at me with those dreadful eyes again. But he wasn't. Instead, in the doorway to the room was someone else. Someone who, by every stretch of the imagination, shouldn't have been there.

Hektor stood assertively at the room's entrance. Blood was smeared on the side of his head from the bullet he'd put into himself, and his black trench coat was still soaked by the storm outside. He walked toward me and I could hear a tiny cackle crop up from somewhere unknown. The doll was watching this whole time. I felt scorned by him yet again. Only this time, something felt different. A strange feeling took control of me. I had seen Hektor die with my own eyes. He placed the trigger to his head and pulled the trigger. He was violently shot to the ground by his own hand. I was hallucinating...this wasn't real. It *couldn't* have been.

My vision grew slightly foggy and the thunderous roars from outside became muffled. I turned my back to the phantom who ominously closed in on me.

"You're not real," I said to myself, but also to Hektor. "None of this is." I heard his footsteps slowly approaching so I closed my eyes and wished away the ghostly horror.

The footsteps grew loud enough to where I was certain Hektor was right behind me, and then they stopped. Silence filled the room and overwhelmed me. I began to shake.

Come see the ghosts for yourself.

The line in the first note didn't disappoint. I had seen the ghosts...*my* ghosts. I was going mad...

Just then, I felt cold fingers on my neck again. A shiver shot through me from head to toe like a ripple-effect. Once they hit the soles of my feet, the cold touch on my neck became warm. It felt like a normal human touch now and not the icy prodding of a ghoul like it first did.

I turned around, now expecting to see consolation; someone who had come to save me from this surreal nightmare and aid in my escape from Castle Shade. But, I didn't. I only saw...Hektor.

I stared into his wearied eyes. Just beneath the glassy surface of them, I could sense a hungry form of skepticism. But for what? What were his eyes studying in mine? Why was he looking back into mine as if he was awaiting some sort of long anticipated revelation?

As I trembled before him in uncertainty, I decided to speak first, admitting to him and myself the most baffling truth. "You're not dead. You didn't really shoot yourself."

Hektor scowled at my remark. His face spasmed as a surge of pain radiated through the superficial wound on the side of his head. He briefly held onto his rigid stare, but then broke the bond with a dispirited smirk and said to himself:

"It didn't work."

Hektor was now visibly distressed. Any sort of skeptical optimism that had plastered his face disappeared just as quickly as his touch to my neck turned warm. He turned away from me and walked to one of the tables that a computer sat on. He rolled a stool to it and sat down, beginning to type belligerently into an already open file on the screen.

He muttered things angrily as he typed with precision. I just stood there in a state of ignorance. Confusion didn't even explain what I was feeling. It felt like everyone had been in on a joke except me. I saw Madison hanging. I watched Symon kill Becca and then chase me through the castle with a bloody axe. Whatever was going on I didn't want to know anymore. I just wanted to leave.

I glanced back at the door which was still open. My nerves vamped up as I prepared to make a move, but Hektor must have known what I was thinking. Coincidentally he looked over his shoulder at the same time I was planning an escape. He pressed a button on a small remote and the door closed on its own. I heard it lock and then I ran to it and desperately tried to turn the knob, but it wouldn't budge.

Hektor turned back to face the computer again without saying a word. I took a couple steps closer toward him, but still kept a heedful distance between us. I was aware now that Hektor was a threat. I just wasn't sure what *kind* of threat.

A boring, run-of-the-mill life forced me to take a risk and investigate the mysteries that Castle Shade concealed. Now, I wish I hadn't. I wish I had stayed in my generic life at home with Kayla and Mark. My desperate curiosity was going to lead to my end.

"What is all this?" I asked, my voice slicing through the silence like a knife.

Hektor wasted no time. He stood up from this stool and removed his trench coat. Underneath, he wore a white lab coat. On the breast pocket, a name was stitched: Dr. Hektor Shade.

"Apparently it's nothing," he said. "I was so close this time. But a flaw is a flaw. It needs to be perfect. Otherwise it's just inane. There is one last resort to get it right though..."

"What are you talking about?"

Hektor fell into a deep thought and whispered to himself, "The failsafe."

He came out of his thoughts and smirked, appearing unhinged now behind his glassy gaze. "Forced Fear," he said. "It's a pheromone my family has been trying to perfect since 1900. The government enlisted my great great grandfather to mold a remedy that would create cerebral disorder amongst the enemy to allow self destruction within their core, rather than having to use violent force from an opposing army."

Hektor turned back to his computer and leaned over it, giving me a moment to fathom what he was talking about. A remedy to create cerebral disorder? It sounded like Forced Fear was a mind control substance commissioned by an outdated government decree. Something that unethical would no longer be legal in this day and age.

I looked to my left and saw a clipboard exhibited on a small table. I leaned over to inspect what was printed on the top page. It was a list of names. At the very top it read:

Subject # 34. Rebecca M. Brown. Age 24. Helminthologist. Resides in Kingston, New York. Originally from Hilliard, Ohio. Forced Fear Method: Polluted Physical Correspondence and Visual Aid. Trigger: Black Worms.

Next on the list was Symon:

Subject #35. Symon C. Clark. Age 31. Divorce Lawyer. Resides in Binghamton, New York. Originally from Doyle Township, Wisconsin. Forced Fear Method: Direct Epidermis and Oral Contact. Trigger: Accused of Multiple Murders.

The third and final name was my own:

*Subject #36. Samuel A. Morris. Age 42. Library
Director. Resides in White Plains, New York.
Originally from Hartford, Connecticut. Forced Fear
Method: Polluted Physical Correspondence and
Visual Aid. Trigger: Engineered 'Ghost House'
Book with Demonic Doll Image.*

With timorous hands, I flipped the page to
the next one. *Madison L. Nash* was printed,
preceded by *Subject #31*. Before I could see
anything else, Hektor appeared beside me. He
placed a hand on my shoulder and startled me
out of my concentration. I released my fingers
from the paper and asked:

"What have you done to us?"

Hektor's response sounded as if it had been
rehearsed to death, hitting only the cliff notes
of a larger explanation:

"Instill novel paranoia, making one
overthink. Introduce the fear trigger to create
an obsessive nature to said trigger. Blend the
subjects for shared mass delusion resulting in
self destructive actions. Those are, and have
always been, the orders," he said. "And this is

the closest any of us have ever come. *You* saw the black worms. *You* saw the doll. *You* saw Symon commiting a grisly murder and then coming for you. Becca and Symon only experienced their own triggers. You, however, were the sole success until you believed I wasn't dead. I should have stayed dead in your eyes. *I should be nothing more than a ghost to you.*"

Once I thought I had figured out what Hektor was doing, I was lost again in a snarl of clashing thoughts. I found myself wondering about Becca and Symon's true fates. Were *they* really dead?

"Where are the others?" I fearfully inquired.

"Symon displayed the destructive nature I've been after, but not the shared delusions. He's flawed, but still has potential. Becca was an unfortunate casualty. I won't get anything out of her now."

"Is Symon dead?" I asked. Hektor had previously told me he was dead, impaled on the bridge outside, yet a ghoulish version of him chased me with an axe. "Is he a ghost?" I repeated.

SCOTT DONNELLY

"He's not a ghost. Although I'm sure there are ghosts here," Hektor said, looking around the room dauntingly. "Too many have died within these walls for there not to be. I've heard things - *voices, breathing* - in here when I *don't* have any subjects running around like blind rats. I'm sure they even help move things along in some way..."

"So Symon really tried to kill me?"

Hektor smirked. "No. He was an apparition triggered by a deliberate marker and then conjured up by sensory conditioning. You believed him to be a murderer, you believed him to be dead — that all worked with you."

Hektor turned around and his calm, yet irritated, demeanor exploded into a sudden vile fury. He picked up the rolling stool and tossed it against the wall.

"If only you believed me to be dead!" he roared in a detonation of rage. *"Why couldn't you just believe it!"*

Hektor was succumbing to a lifetime of repeated scientific catastrophes. His eyes no longer looked weary, but enraged. The Shade family legacy had been built solely on the fruition of Forced Fear, but each generation continued to fail. I thought back to the second letter that arrived at my home:

In this house of ghosts, truths will be discovered and lives will be changed, for life in this house is nothing more than an appraisal.

This entire scenario had been strategically orchestrated from the start. The three of us were somehow chosen to be the ill-starred subjects of this latest trial at Castle Shade...**a house that will fulfill the desires of a mad brain.** Hektor *was* that mad brain. He was a desperate and obsessed scientist — a true *mad scientist*. There was no longer a legit purpose for Forced Fear aside from an insane family's need to get it right.

Fear began to consume me again, knocking my composure off balance. My stomach twisted in knots as I worried I would never step foot outside of Castle Shade again. The questions I had began to ravage my mind; my head throbbed in agony. I felt sick, I felt uncomfortable, I felt disturbed.

Hektor leaned back over his computer and pulled up another screen, an email. He began to type until half the document was filled with his words. I didn't know what he was writing, which only added to my anxious curiosity. He seemed to finish the email quickly and then clicked a button that sent it away. Whatever he wrote went somewhere, to someone unknown.

"What are you doing?" I hollered. Hektor didn't respond. He picked up the remote that had closed and locked the door to the lab. He unlatched the back of it and removed the motherboard. He walked it over to the tub of the lucid pheromone. He dropped it in and I watched an electric current fry the circuits.

The door wouldn't open without that remote.; that was my only way out. Everything that happened next unraveled very quickly. Hektor looked around the lab, methodically checking all the boxes: he snipped the computer wires with scissors, unlocked a single door against the far wall that I assumed to be a closet and then pulled his snub nose revolver from his pocket. That's when my paranoia began to hit hard.

"Hektor?" I sternly addressed him. He was refusing to answer me or even acknowledge my presence anymore. "What are you doing?"

Hektor emptied the blanks that remained in the gun and then opened a desk drawer, pulling out a single chrome bullet. He carefully loaded it into the revolver and locked it in place.

Everything stopped after that. He approached me but I was too afraid to move. I could hear my teeth chattering and felt the anxious throbbing of my heart against my ribs. As Hektor looked deep into my eyes, I noticed that *his* were black and empty.

"Failsafe," he whispered in my face.

"What are you talking about?"

Hektor smiled. His teeth were grainy and a couple were chipped. The pores on his face were huge and sharp gray hairs stood erect sporadically across his chin and cheeks. He was a tired man in his last act.

"I'll be right back. Listen for me knocking and then let me in," he hissed.

I nodded rapidly, not completely understanding his bizarre request, but nervous as hell with the gun shaking in his grip.

"Do you understand?" he asked.

I nodded.

Hektor smiled. "Good." In a flash, Hektor lifted the gun to his head and pulled the trigger again. The explosion from the muzzle blinded me and my face was sprayed with a warm liquid. I heard Hektor crumble to the floor, followed by a large splash. I dropped to my knees. The ringing was so loud I felt like *my* head was going to explode as well. I kept my eyes clamped shut until the ringing subsided and then reluctantly opened them.

Red was all I could see. It was splattered on me, the walls, the tables and floor. The inside of Hektor's skull was exposed, oozing blood and brain matter. The mad brain was now free from its warped confines. The plastic tub that once held the pheromone was upside down and on the floor next to him. The liquid had spilled everywhere.

I immediately stood up and ran for the door, trying desperately to open it. But it was no use. Whatever mechanism held it shut had been disabled after Hektor drowned the remote's circuits. I turned around and scanned the

room. There had to be another way out. I spied
the door against the far wall that Hektor had
unlocked. I raced across the room and opened
it. Inside was nothing; an empty closet. Why
did he unlock it? I walked into the small
pantry-sized room and felt the walls. They were
seamless and made of metal. I banged on all
three of the inner walls.

"Hello?" I called out. "Is anyone there?" I
stepped back from the closet but kept looking
in. I didn't know exactly what I expected to see.
Any last sliver of hope I had was in that closet,
so to look away and accept it as a dead end was
dispiriting.

I slowly turned around once more to take in
the whole scope of the room. The bloody body
of Hektor Shade lay on the floor in front of me.
The pheromone vapors rose into the air as I
continued to breathe heavily. A cackle
reverberated from somewhere. I could hear the
squishing of the hellish worms in my ears and
now I could even feel them behind my eyes. I
felt Symon's murderous presence awaiting the
escape from the room that would never
happen.

And then, the knocking started. I turned back and faced the metal closet. The knocks came slow at first, sounding like a railroad spike being hammered in slow motion. It grew louder and more hasty, competing with the erratic pulsation of my heart.

Hektor was back. Just as he had promised.

EPILOGUE
OF THE MAD HORRORS

*I*t is a house that called me. A house of darkness that will continue to fulfill the desires of a mad brain. It is a house that haunts me with its ghosts; *my* ghosts and the many that still lurk within its wickedness. They scratch and claw through my fragile hide, bringing madness of all kinds bubbling to the surface. I came to see the ghosts for myself.

In this house of madness, murder and insanity, many lives have changed, including mine. My life now is nothing more than a sick, measureless trial.

Time became an irrelevance the longer I remained in the lab. Days, a week - two weeks - I didn't even know and it didn't matter anymore. The prickly stubble on my face had begun its transformation into a bushy and uncomfortable beard. My eyes were sore from a vicious back and forth of fatigue and tears. My body was weak, hungry and dehydrated.

The body of Dr. Hektor Shade lay decomposing in the room in the exact spot he had dropped dead. Everytime I tried to approach him, his knocking became more hostile, like he was warning me of yet another unfathomable danger; one in which I couldn't possibly comprehend prior to its inevitable reveal.

*Oh, the knocking...*once it started, it didn't stop. It was a constant background ambience that I became so used to that sometimes I didn't even realize it was still occuring. Hektor made sure his presence was known at all times. Warning, threatening — each knock meant something different. Each one planted seeds of doubt, curious implications and spine-chilling angst. I couldn't leave because of Symon outside the door. I couldn't stay because of the doll, ceaselessly gawking at me with malice from every shadow in the lab. The electricity had failed days ago, stimulating a red glow from the generator lights and disclosing more ominous shadows than I cared to know existed. Each one sheltered the doll, but whether or not it was a callous titter, glowing eyes or a guttural wail that it unveiled, regularly changed. It liked to keep me on my toes.

The worms, however, I had been able to keep at bay. I came to the conclusion that they didn't like the cold entrapment of being in the metal closet. So that's where I stayed. They wouldn't cross the threshold as long as I didn't. They squelched and squirmed just outside the door, giving me my entertainment and reminding me of Becca. Becca reminded me of Symon. Symon reminded me of—

A distinct clicking sound drew my attention across the room and to the primary door of the lab. The locking mechanism shifted and then with an echoing bang, it detached from the wall and the door creaked open.

"Symon?" I called out, standing to my feet, but not brave enough to cross the worm's barricade.

The door opened more and a figure entered the room. Shrouded in the shadows and red haze, the figure immediately covered his or her mouth and nose. I was sure the stench of Dr. Shade was to blame for that. I was also sure that the figure did not hold an axe, bringing me a sense of comfort in knowing that it wasn't Symon. In fact, this person was a little shorter and much more spindly.

"Who is that?" I called out. The figure stepped further into the room and ignited a flashlight. With the broader shoulders and short hair, I assumed it to be a male. "Can you get me out of here?" I pleaded. "I need to get home to my family."

The man pointed the flashlight down at Hektor's body and then directly at me. My vision was compromised by the beaming glare and I half covered my eyes with my hands. As I forced my eyes to adjust, the man moved in closer.

"Who are you?" I asked. My knees began to shake and then gave out underneath the crippling condition my body had adopted since the failsafe began. The man stopped only inches from me and then knelt down so we were eye level. He adjusted the flashlight and I could now see his face.

He was a young, handsome man. He was dressed sharply with a leather satchel draped over his shoulder. His hair was slickly gelled and he smelled of a musky cologne. His eyes were piercing blue and his growing smile was genuine. I knew this man. I *worked* with this man.

"*Tim?*" I struggled to believe my eyes.

"Mr. Morris, is my uncle dead?" he asked.

"What?" I questioned.

Tim moved out of the way and aimed his light on the decaying body of Dr. Shade. "My uncle," he repeated. "Is he dead?"

Tim returned his attention to me and his smile evaporated. The nice young man was gone and in his place was someone with a consequential agenda.

"Tim, what are you doing here? How did you—"

I suddenly remembered him arriving at the library. He was looking for work and had been recommended by an extended family member on Kayla's side...*Madison*. He worked briefly as a handyman for her before she sent him my way.

"Did you bring Madison here, too?" I begged to know. My emotions had started to creep up on me and my shaking became excessive. Tim only smirked at my question and then returned to his serious demeanor.

He repeated once more, slowly, and rashly, "Is my uncle dead?"

"Dr. Shade?"

Tim nodded.

I took a deep breath, once again inhaling the putrid air that filled the laboratory and wondered: *What kind of question was that.*

"No," I said. My eyes wandered around the metallic closet I concealed myself in. I heard a knock here and a knock there. It was coming from the other side of the walls. It was coming from Tim's uncle, Dr. Hektor Shade. "He's everywhere," I said with a quake in my voice.

Tim smirked and stood to his feet. From the leather satchel he carried, he extracted a book and tossed it down to my feet. He briefly shined his light onto the book's cover: *Ghost House.*

"Here's a little reading material for you to stimulate your imagination. I'll go find you some playthings," Tim balefully smirked as the words left his lips.

My eyes were instantly glued to the book's cover and the details stood out more than they had the first time. The large, gothic house on the cover was clearly that of Castle Shade. The doll's hypnotizing eyes were the same ones that had incessantly vexed me: I was in the *Ghost House*, surrounded by the dead, the depraved - my life was nothing now but a warped and vile appraisal.

From the bowels of the castle, the chilling cackle rose up again, more clamorous than it had ever been. The knocking on the walls that surrounded me reverberated through my bones and the sloshing of the repulsive mass before me reiterated our unjust agreement. The sound of the door lock echoed through the laboratory and that's when I realized Tim was gone, replaced once more by Symon on the other side.

Tim had left me alone with the unceasing horrors dwelling within Castle Shade. But as the cackle, the knocking, the squirming and stalking congested my ill brain, I realized something:

I was now one of the mad horrors forever entombed in Castle Shade. I hope my playthings play nice.

THE EMAIL

*T*he sun had set in eastern Pennsylvania, bringing an autumn chill creeping into the air. The woods behind a row of houses on Beaker Street were the setting of a massive search for a missing person. Officers and search party volunteers shined flashlights through the wilderness, calling out the name "Madison!" as much as they could. Some of the callers began to go hoarse from the tenacious shouting. Their gruff voices echoed through the trees, and the crunching of leaves from the dozens of people sounded like a constant static.

Kayla and Mark Morris walked side by side, nervous and quieter than the rest of the search party. Kayla clenched her son's arm, afraid to let go; afraid she'd lose someone else. They were looking for Madison Nash, Kayla's younger sister. She was last seen jogging through the neighborhood and along the treeline of the wooded area behind her home on Beaker Street. That was two days earlier. No one had seen or heard from her since.

Kayla assumed the worst, something she wouldn't normally do. But her brain was working overtime. Her thoughts were manic and bestrewed, forking off in countless directions, but always coalesced into one grim depiction. It was one of Madison, drenched in the gore of an irreversible and odious act.

Just as it wasn't like Kayla to have such a blinkered thought, it also wasn't like Madison to vanish into thin air. She had a job, a comfortable life in the mountainous valleys of Pennsylvania - it didn't make sense to just leave it all. Kayla couldn't shake the thought of her little sister turning up dead. She *knew* it was morbid to think, but she couldn't help it. Something told her it was the only truth.

Mark pulled out his phone with his free hand and looked for a text from his father. There was nothing. There hadn't been for hours. Just continuous failed sends from Mark's end of things.

"He said he was on his way, right?" Mark asked his mother.

She just nodded, staring off into space as they walked. The constant calling and shouting of her sister's name was weighing heavily on her. Each time Madison's name was uttered, the pit of her stomach felt more and more hollow. She took this as proof of the grisly fate she knew her sister had faced.

"Something's wrong," Mark quietly said as he stuffed the phone back into his pocket. He swallowed, nerves steadily swelling inside of him. He was filled with a fear of not knowing where his father was. He was filled with doubt of his safety...he was filled with guilt for leaving the skull in his room. The skull was home, where they had last left his father. The skull's agenda was a secret; even Mark didn't know what it was. It wouldn't tell him. It wouldn't even give the slightest clue. But in the abyss of the skull's marrow, only a cold and dangerous agenda could thrive.

An officer rushed past Kayla and Mark, joining two others and quietly whispering to one another. Kayla focused her curiosity on the three members of law enforcement, wondering what new development had their attention and why it was such a secret.

Were they discussing the morbidity of Madison's remains? The grisly manner in which she was murdered? Did they have the sick fiend in custody? Was there even enough of Madison left to identify?

"I wonder why they just wont tell us," Kayla said to Mark. Mark didn't respond, but did look to acknowledge the strange pow-wow.

Someone, another member of the search party, walked up beside Kayla and Mark. It was a young man, dressed warmly for the night time search. The hood to his coat was over his head, and his hands were stuffed into his pockets. His closeness roused Kayla's attention, and she looked at him, peeved.

She recognized him, but couldn't think of where from. He studied his face. He was a young, good-looking man. He was cleanly shaven and Kayla could smell a faint, yet pleasant, cologne on him.

Where do I know him from? Kayla thought to herself. And then, it hit her. His name was Tim. She had briefly met him at the library where Sam worked.

"Tim?" she asked out loud. Tim turned and looked at Kayla. He smiled at her.

"Hi," he said.

Kayla remembered even more now. He had done some work around Madison's house. He fixed a few pipes and reattached some siding. She remembered Madison's attraction to him, despite her being at least ten years older than the handsome handyman. He confided in her, possibly even flirting and stringing her along to a relationship that would never happen. His father had died, and Tim needed work to pay off some of his debt. He needed a more steady job, so Madison had recommended him to Sam.

There was a position open at the library, and
Sam jumped at the chance to help someone
who needed it.

"What are you doing here? Aren't you still
working at the library in White Plains?" Kayla
asked.

Tim nodded. "I am. I heard about Madison
and wanted to help."

Kayla certainly wasn't in the right state of
mind, but she did find it odd that Tim - a
handyman who only *briefly* worked for her
sister - would make a two-hour road trip to
help look for her. Some would even call it
suspicious.

"I'm sorry about your sister," Tim said. "I
hope she's found safely."

Kayla vigorously shook her head, refusing to
allow herself the hope of a happy ending. "She's
dead, I know it. She suffered horribly. The
police don't know it yet, but we're looking for a
body."

Tim nodded, paying close attention to
Kayla's paranoia-ridden ramblings. She wasn't
thinking with any kind of pragmatic hope. She
had jumped to the worst possible resolution.

From Tim's research, he could tell this wasn't Kayla's normal, rational thought process.

The pheromone was working.

Tim noticed Mark's demeanor as well. He looked scared; anxious about something. He was silent and seemed to sink deeper into the growing contortion of his nebulous mind.

It was working with him as well.

To have the trio of subjects back at the castle, confined and primed for conflict was one thing - *it was routine* - but to have two other subjects in the wild and amongst ingenuous spectators, the potential hazards were incalculable. The fuses that had been lit could fulminate at any given moment, and this was just the emotive addition the Forced Fear experiment needed.

As the hollow search for Madison Nash continued in the cold wilderness, Tim's phone buzzed against his hand in his pocket. He pulled it from his jeans and saw an email notification. It was from his uncle, and the email subject was simply labeled: *Failsafe Initiated.*

There was a moment of silence in Tim's mind. The failsafe was the endmost effort of any trial conducted with regard to Forced Fear. It was in the decades-old fine print. The initiation of the failsafe confirmed one thing for sure: Tim's uncle was dead. It was an audacious measure to take, although bleak, but it did promise a chance at success. Probably even the closest chance yet. His uncle would have never initiated the failsafe if he didn't believe in its payoff.

Tim turned away from Kayla and Mark, and opened the email. It was on the shorter side, much shorter than the routine reports his father used to send. But, one when brother died, the other took control. The differences between their work weren't extreme; they both had an unwavering dedication to the coda.

Tim dimmed his phone's light and read the posthumous narrative arranged before his eyes:

Dear Tim,

I have initiated the failsafe. This is goodbye between us. You are no longer just a recruiter, but are the sole experimenter, the last of the Shade family. Unless you pave the way for future offspring to take